QUEEN OF DARKNESS

TONY BRADMAN

BLOOMSBURY EDUCATION
LONDON OXFORD NEW YORK NEW DELHI SYDNEY

For Sally, my very own Iceni goddess

CONTENTS

CHAPTER ONE

The Roman Way

The Royal Place of the Iceni, Eastern Britain, 60 CE

The winter sun was low in the sky when Rhianna burst out of the roundhouse, pulling her little sister Eleri along behind her. Rhianna stomped off up the muddy track, away from the house that had been their home for as long as she could remember, keeping hold of Eleri and ignoring the stares of their neighbours.

Most of them had come out of their houses to listen to the row that had just taken place.

'Where are we going, Rhianna?' said Eleri. 'It will be dark soon.'

'I know that,' said Rhianna. 'We're going to speak to the king.'

'But I don't want to go anywhere in the dark,' said Eleri, dragging her heels, trying to hold Rhianna back. 'I want to be inside, by the fire. I want my supper.'

Rhianna halted and turned to face her sister. 'Stop whining, Eleri!' she snapped, the fury of the argument still surging through her like a river in full flood after the rain. 'Didn't you hear Magunna? Our stepmother has thrown us out, which means there might not be any supper for either of us tonight, or perhaps ever again. So unless I do something about it, we're going to starve to death. *Do you understand me?*'

'Yes, Rhianna,' Eleri whispered, her bottom lip quivering. She was seven summers old and small for her age, and so was Rhianna, who was five summers older. Rhianna had her father's coarse red hair, a great tangle of it that she kept tied back, but Eleri had the same black hair as their mother. Their eyes were different colours too, Rhianna's a bright cornflower-blue, Eleri's as brown as the fur of an otter.

Tears filled Eleri's eyes now, and Rhianna's heart softened. She had always felt close to her sister, had always wanted to protect her from harm. Rhianna hugged Eleri, and felt her trembling like a frightened puppy. The cold wasn't helping, Rhianna realised with a pang of guilt. In her anger she had not stopped to find Eleri's warm winter cloak before she had stormed out, scooping up her sister with her. The two of them were only wearing thin tunics and leggings, and that certainly wasn't enough in this bitter air.

'I'm sorry, Eleri,' she said quietly, kissing the top of her sister's head and catching her familiar scent. 'I shouldn't have said all that; I'm just upset. You know how angry Magunna makes me… Don't worry, I'll make sure you get some supper tonight. I've never let you down, have I?'

'No, you haven't,' Eleri said. 'But what's happened is bad, isn't it?'

Rhianna didn't give her sister an answer. She held her for a while longer, then took her hand and started up the track again. There was no point in telling Eleri she was right, Rhianna thought – things were *very* bad. Their only hope was to seek justice from King Prasutagus. She knew the people of the tribe did that sometimes, when they couldn't settle a dispute between themselves. Rhianna would tell the king how unfair their stepmother was being, and ask him to take their side.

They hurried on, through the lower part of the Royal Place, with its houses crammed together. Tracks snaked between them, and smoke rose from the holes in the middle of their conical thatched roofs. Eventually they came to the Meeting Ground, a great open space where a thousand people would gather to celebrate festivals or hear important news. From there you could look out over the whole settlement.

The Royal Place of the Iceni was surrounded by a deep ditch and a mound of earth topped with

4

a stockade of tall wooden stakes. There was only one way in, and gates that could be sealed shut with the trimmed trunk of an oak blocked that. Beyond were wide fields of wheat and barley, and pastures where people grazed their horses and the cattle and sheep that gave them milk, cheese and meat. Further off, beyond the fields, was a broad river that led to the marshes one way and the sea the other.

On the far side of the Meeting Ground stood the most important buildings. To the left was the King's House. It was much bigger than an ordinary roundhouse, its outside made of thick logs the height of a man, its roof rising even higher. To the right was the Queen's House, which was slightly smaller. Between them stood another structure, the Feast House. That was where they would find the king – he and the queen usually met there at this time of day for the evening meal.

The doors of the Feast House were wide open and warm red light from the hearth-fire within spilled on to the mud outside. A guard usually stood watch at the doors, but tonight nobody was there to keep Rhianna and Eleri out. Nevertheless, Rhianna ducked inside quickly and she and Eleri kept to the shadows to begin with. She held her finger over her lips and Eleri nodded silently to show she understood.

The Feast House was for the king and queen and the important people in the tribe, and Rhianna and her sister had never been inside before. Rhianna had peeked through the doorway more than once though, so what she saw now was familiar. The hearth-fire lay at the centre of the large circular space, with smoke from its burning logs coiling lazily to the roof-hole above. A servant was roasting a sheep on a spit over the fire, the fat dripping and hissing as it fell into the flames. The smell made Rhianna's mouth water.

There was room for many to gather in the Feast House – bright rugs and cushions stuffed with dried bracken were scattered around the hearth. But Rhianna soon realised the voices she could hear belonged to a small number of people, no more than a dozen. They were reclining on couches, leaning on their elbows, eating and drinking from a long table covered in dishes and cups. A few servants were there to attend them, and oil lamps hung from the roof beams above, like stars shining in the night sky.

Rhianna recognised King Prasutagus and the men around him, his bodyguards. All of them were wearing long white tunics that hung well below their knees. Rhianna knew this was the style of the Romans, the invaders who had conquered much of Britannia nearly twenty years ago, in the time of their Emperor Claudius.

Many people – even in the free lands – admired the Romans and tried to copy them. Eating from couches was a habit of rich Romans, apparently. Most of the Iceni sat cross-legged around the hearth to eat, and didn't stuff themselves either. Yet King Prasutagus clearly ate far too much. He had a fat stomach and his face rolled over his neck in a series of wobbly chins. He was old, with thin grey hair cut close to his scalp, and he was clean-shaven in the Roman way. Iceni men usually grew their hair long and had a thick moustache that hung down on either side of their chin.

Some people in the Royal Place laughed at Prasutagus behind his back, but nobody made fun of Boudica, the queen, or Heart of the Iceni as queens had always been called in the tribe. Rhianna glanced at her now. Although she'd seen the queen many times before, it had only ever been in the distance. Now, she saw Boudica sitting upright on a couch, apart from her husband, her long red hair tumbling over her shoulders, a look of boredom and distaste on her beautiful face. She wore a green gown of the finest wool, thick golden bracelets on her wrists and a great golden torc around her pale neck.

Rhianna stepped out of the shadows and walked with Eleri towards the couches. A couple of the men glanced at them, but the king kept talking, unaware that the sisters were standing in front of him. For a moment Rhianna struggled to understand what he was saying, and then realised he was speaking Latin, the language of the Romans. She knew that was another thing admirers of the Romans did. Most of the king's bodyguards spoke Latin, or liked to give the impression they could. But all of them were rough and brutal, and they were very unpopular in the Royal Place.

'Lord Prasutagus,' Rhianna said as loudly as she dared, hoping he hadn't forgotten his own language, the ancient tongue of the Iceni. 'I come to you seeking justice.'

Silence fell in the Feast House, and all eyes turned to Rhianna and Eleri.

'Be off with you, girl,' said Prasutagus, speaking in the Iceni tongue. He frowned irritably and waved her away. 'I am not in a listening mood this evening.'

'Please, I beg you to hear me, Lord!' said Rhianna. 'Our evil stepmother Magunna has thrown us out of our home, and that's not fair, she has no right to do so…'

'Yes, yes, you've probably got a long list of grievances,' said Prasutagus. 'But I have no desire to hear them now – I'm sure they would give me indigestion!'

He laughed at his joke and his bodyguards joined in. Eleri started to cry again, and Rhianna felt hot tears prickling in her own eyes. She *had* to get the king's attention… Suddenly she remembered the prayer her mother had always used when she wanted something badly. 'My lord,' Rhianna said, more loudly this time, 'I ask you in the sacred name of the Morrigan, the triple goddess, to listen to my plea…'

'Blessed be the goddess,' said the queen, her voice cutting through the men's laughter. 'She who is all the stages of a woman's life in one – young girl, mother and old woman. I will listen to you in her name, even if my husband will not.'

Silence fell once more. Rhianna turned to look at the queen and their eyes met – Boudica's were the green of her gown. A faint smile played upon her lips.

'Now, Boudica, don't…' Prasutagus began. The queen turned her gaze on him and he quickly raised his hands in surrender, palms outwards. 'Fine, as you wish…'

Rhianna thought it best to keep her story short. She gave the queen their names, and told her that their mother Doleda had died two winters ago, having been sickly for several years. Rhianna had done her best to look after her as well as Eleri, which was why Rhianna had no friends of her own age. Their father Esico had soon taken Magunna as his new wife, and she had hated Rhianna and Eleri right from the start. They had hated her in return, but their father had managed to stop them arguing too much. Then he was killed in a chariot race at the last Summer Gathering.

Every year the whole tribe gathered at the Royal Place in the summer, with people coming from the outlying settlements to gossip and feast and enjoy themselves in games and races. Rhianna had always loved those days, but when she thought of them now, all she could see in her mind's eye was the crash that had killed her father. Another man had driven his chariot recklessly across his path, making him swerve. Her father's chariot had flipped over and he had died instantly. Everyone said it had been an unlucky accident, the kind of thing that could happen in any race.

'Yes, I remember,' said the queen. 'As usual, the young men were showing off, trying to impress the girls with their bravery, and your father paid the price. I suppose this wretched Magunna then felt free to make you two pay a price as well?'

'She has treated us like slaves, my lady,' said Rhianna. 'And today she threatened to beat my sister. I told her I would kill her if she did, so she threw us out of the only home we have ever known. We have nowhere to go, no kin to take us in.'

The queen's smile returned to her lips. 'I think we share more than the colour of our hair, Rhianna, daughter of Doleda,' she said. 'I would have done the same.'

'The girl said *what* to her stepmother?' spluttered the king. 'I think...'

'Be quiet, Prasutagus,' said the queen. 'Nobody wants to know what you think. I will decide what

12

happens here.' She looked once more at Rhianna and Eleri. 'You cannot return to your former home,' she said. 'Let your stepmother have it.'

'What about us?' said Rhianna, her heart sinking. 'Where are we to live?'

'Why, with me,' said the queen. 'But only if you want to, of course.'

Rhianna was stunned, and for a moment she could not speak.

So she nodded eagerly instead.

CHAPTER TWO

Fierce-Looking Women

After a while, the queen rose from her couch to leave the Feast House, bidding Rhianna and Eleri to follow her. Prasutagus watched them go, a look of amusement on his face. 'Leaving so soon, my love?' he called out. 'And without even a goodnight kiss for your lord and master!' The bodyguards laughed and Rhianna glanced at the queen to see how she would react. Boudica simply ignored them.

The air had grown colder outside and the Royal Place was full of darkness, with only a white sliver of moon and a sprinkling of stars in the sky to light their way. Rhianna held Eleri close, but it was just a short walk to the Queen's House, and once they were inside, warmth folded around them like a blanket. The hearth was bigger than that of the Feast House, and the logs gave off a sweet smell as they burned.

'Sit here, by the fire,' said the queen, pulling up a pair of thick, bracken-stuffed cushions for the girls. 'We'd better get you fed. Tegan! Maeve! Where are you?'

Rhianna sat down, with Eleri snuggled in beside her. It was hard to believe they were actually inside the Queen's House, Rhianna thought, yet it was true.

There were fewer lamps than in the Feast House, and the shadows were thicker. Rhianna saw strange shapes hanging from the roof beams, and realised they were bundles of dried herbs, stoppered pots and jars, strings of bird feathers, animal skulls. The queen was well known for making powerful healing salves and potions to cure illnesses.

Two young women appeared out of the shadows. Boudica's daughters were older than Rhianna – Tegan perhaps eighteen summers and Maeve fifteen. They both looked like their mother, although Maeve was small and slight and her hair was less fiery. They both had open, friendly faces and were dressed in fine woollen gowns. Tegan's was the bright red of holly berries in winter and Maeve's was a deep blue.

'Ask the servants to fetch food and drink for our new friends,' said the queen. 'Rhianna and her little sister Eleri will be living with us from now on.'

'Of course,' said Tegan, smiling at them. 'There's some stew, I think…'

The stew was brought to them in bowls, and there was bread as well, and mare's milk with honey. Rhianna gave her sister a nudge, as if to say *I told you I'd make sure you got some supper tonight*, but Eleri was already eating and didn't notice. Rhianna smiled and started eating too, the food warming her more than the fire.

'So… who taught you about the goddess?' said the queen at last. She was sitting beside the sisters, the light of the hearth flames dancing in her eyes and glinting off her torc and bracelets. 'She has been forgotten by the tribe since the Romans came.'

'Our mother,' said Rhianna. 'She was not of the Iceni, but of the Brigantes. Our father was restless as a young man and they met when he was on his travels in the north. Mother always swore by the goddess and taught us to do the same.'

'Ah, that would explain it,' said the queen, smiling. 'Women still have power among the Brigantes. Even the Romans are scared of their queen, Cartimandua. And yet the men of our tribe refuse to worship the goddess as they used to…'

Each tribe had its own ways, and there had often been cattle raids between them, or even war. But according to Rhianna's mother, at one time every tribe in the island of Britannia had worshipped the goddess and each was ruled by a powerful queen. Now it was just the Brigantes who still lived like this. There had been kings, but a man had to marry a queen to become one – and queens chose their husbands. But then the men in many tribes had begun to turn against the goddess, and worship lesser gods in their own image. Soon there were even men-priests called Druids, and wherever they seized power they ended the rule of women. Only a few tribes kept the Druids out, the Iceni among them.

But change had come to the Iceni too. Boudica had chosen her first husband Conor, the father of her daughters, just as queens of the Iceni had always done. But he had died fighting the Romans when they had come up from the south thirteen summers ago. The Romans had won, but they had agreed to let the tribe remain free – if they upheld certain conditions. They said the Iceni had to pay them a 'tribute' every year. This was to be made up of many gold and silver coins, ten wagonloads of wheat and ten of barley, a hundred fine horses and the same number of cattle and sheep.

The Romans had also declared that the tribe must be ruled by a king. They chose Prasutagus because he had spent many years in their lands across the sea – in Gaul, mostly, but he often boasted that he had visited the city of Rome itself. He was more Roman in his beliefs than Iceni, and the Romans knew he would follow their ways. They believed that only men should rule, and although they worshipped some goddesses, their most powerful gods – such as Jupiter and Mars – were male. The nobles of the tribe agreed that they must do what the Romans wanted, and told Boudica she had to marry him.

Rhianna remembered her mother and father arguing about it often – her father saying it was right for men to rule because they were warriors, her mother saying that women were better rulers, and could also be fierce warriors. Suddenly Rhianna felt her eyes prickling with hot tears. Thinking about her parents had opened a great black hole of grief within her and she tumbled into it, wishing they were still alive, knowing they were gone forever. She dropped her bowl and let her tears flow.

'Hush, child,' said Boudica, pulling her close. Rhianna glanced at Eleri and saw that her sister was asleep, curled on the cushion, clutching her empty bowl. 'As soon as I heard you call on the goddess, I knew it was a sign – she has brought us together for a reason, Rhianna,' the queen said softly. 'It must have been hard for you, but your dark time is over. You and your sister will be safe with me, I swear…'

Rhianna let herself be held, and soon she was asleep beside her sister.

* * *

For Rhianna the next few days seemed like a dream come true, or like one of the stories told round the hearth on cold winter nights to make everyone smile, a tale of rags to riches, of despair turned to joy. The queen gave Rhianna and Eleri new clothes, beautiful gowns like those Tegan and Maeve wore, and their own special sleeping place, with blankets and thick furs to wrap themselves in at night. They ate well too, as Boudica's daughters delighted in bringing them the best food.

On the morning of the fifth day, Rhianna approached the queen. Boudica was sitting by the hearth, talking to one of the young women who also lived in her house. Rhianna had noticed the women straight away. There were a dozen of them, all beautiful, but fierce-looking as well. She had asked Tegan about them, and she had said they were just body servants to the queen. But Rhianna felt they were more than that – they were like wolves who had magically been transformed into women.

'My lady…' Rhianna said nervously. 'Would it be all right if I went back to my old house today? We left some things behind that I would like to collect.'

The queen and the young woman stopped talking and turned to her. 'You don't have to ask my permission, Rhianna,' said the queen. 'You can come and go as you please. We Iceni are still mostly a free people – isn't that right, Garwen?'

'We are, and proud of it,' said the young woman, her voice warm and strong. Garwen had clear blue eyes and black hair, and wore an ash-coloured gown.

'Mind you, I have a feeling you might need a little help with that stepmother of yours…'

said the queen. 'I think you'd better go with Rhianna, Garwen.'

Rhianna almost said it wasn't necessary, and that she could handle Magunna herself. But then she thought, why not? She had always faced her stepmother alone and it would be good to have support, especially from someone like Garwen. So she thanked the queen and went to check on her sister. Eleri was more than happy to stay with Maeve, the two of them having taken a liking to each other.

Soon Rhianna and Garwen were walking through the Royal Place, the muddy tracks busy with people and squawking hens, a dog barking in the distance. It was a bright winter's day with a sharp, cold breeze coming from the west, so Rhianna was glad of her new cloak. How strange that life could change so swiftly, she thought. Five days ago she and her sister had walked in the opposite direction, cast out of their home with nothing. Rhianna smiled. Magunna was in for a surprise…

It turned out, however, that Rhianna was in for a surprise herself. She didn't bother to knock on the doorpost like a stranger when she arrived at her old home, and just pushed through the cowhide door-covering. Inside, Magunna was sitting by the hearth, kneading flatbread dough on a wooden board, with smoke from the burning logs curling in the light streaming down through the roof-hole. But someone else was sitting by the hearth: a man called Segovax, a friend of Rhianna's father. Segovax was big and fair and Rhianna had never liked him much. She had liked him even less after the Summer Gathering – he had been the one driving the chariot that had made her father swerve.

Magunna scowled, but Segovax only glanced at Rhianna and concentrated on eating the flatbread he had just taken from a stone at the edge of the hearth. Rhianna felt Garwen push through the door-covering to stand a little way behind her.

'You didn't waste much time, did you?' said Rhianna, glaring at Magunna. 'I should have realised you were up to something. You wanted us out so you could move this pig in. How could you? It's because of him that our father died.'

Segovax paused in his steady chewing and turned to stare at Rhianna with narrowed eyes. He always wore tunics without sleeves so he could show off his arms, with their bulging muscles covered in swirling blue tattoos from shoulder to wrist.

'So what? You can't do anything about it,' Magunna said, smirking. She had scraggy black hair, mean eyes and thin lips. Rhianna had never understood why her father liked her. 'What do you want, anyway? And who's your friend?'

'I want the things that belong to Eleri and me,' said Rhianna, ignoring her second question. Garwen said nothing, but she did step forward. 'Our mother's jewels,' said Rhianna. 'Her rings, the keepsakes she brought with her from the north.'

'What, these?' said Magunna, raising her hands and grinning. She was wearing several rings as well as a silver bracelet, all of which Rhianna recognised as her mother's. 'Well, you can forget it. They're mine, whether you like it or not.'

'Oh no, they're not,' Rhianna said, her voice rising. 'Give them to me, or…'

'Or what, little girl?' growled Segovax. He had finished eating and slowly rose to his feet. 'I think you and your friend had better leave before you get hurt.'

He advanced on Rhianna and Garwen until he loomed over them, his arms outstretched, a big grin on his face. Rhianna backed towards the door, but suddenly Garwen ducked to one side and kicked out at the man's legs, sweeping them from under him. Segovax crashed to the floor and Garwen knelt down, grabbing his hair and pulling back his head. Rhianna was shocked to see that she had a dagger in her hand, and that she was pressing the blade hard against the side of his throat.

Magunna screamed and Garwen looked up at her. 'I am Garwen, body servant to the queen. But more importantly, I have a knife at your man's throat. And I will cut it wide open unless you give Rhianna what is rightfully hers. Quickly now.'

Magunna didn't argue and soon Rhianna had what she had come for. She took a few other things too – an old silver ring of her father's, her mother's comb, and a little bone-handled knife her mother had always used when preparing food.

Garwen released Segovax at last and he sat up, rubbing a cut on his neck.

'Ready, Rhianna?' said Garwen, and Rhianna nodded. They turned to leave, but Rhianna couldn't help taking one last look before she went out of the door.

Magunna stood by the hearth, her eyes burning with more hatred than ever.

CHAPTER THREE

Tremor of Fear

On their way back to the Queen's House, Rhianna could hardly keep her eyes off Garwen. It had been amazing to see her dealing like that with Segovax, a man who was far bigger and stronger than her – she had made it look so easy! But there had also been something dark and scary about what had happened. Rhianna felt sure Garwen really would have cut Segovax's throat without a second thought.

'Come on, out with it,' said Garwen at last. They had reached the Meeting Ground and were walking across it. 'You've been staring at me for so long it's a wonder you haven't tripped and fallen on your face. What is it that you want to ask?'

'Lots of things,' said Rhianna. The wind was colder now, the sky was filling with dark clouds, and it felt as if a storm was brewing. 'How did you *do* that? Could you teach me? And where did you get that dagger? I didn't see you carrying it earlier.'

'So many questions!' Garwen smiled. 'I am a body servant of the queen, and we have all sworn to protect her. So we learn the skills that will help us do that.' She looked Rhianna up and down and shrugged. 'I might be able to teach you, I suppose. I was small and skinny when I was your age... The dagger? For now we keep our weapons hidden. But the day might come when we will be able to wear them openly.'

'Is that because of the Romans? I know they won't allow the men to have swords or shields or daggers or war-spears, only bows and spears for hunting…'

This was something her father had often complained bitterly about. How could men truly be men if they couldn't have weapons and practise with them? Prasutagus had done his best to make sure they didn't, though – anyone he suspected hiding weapons of war had their house ransacked from top to bottom. But his bodyguards had never found any, and of course they were allowed to carry weapons themselves.

'I am not frightened of the Romans. They think women are weak and helpless, so they don't believe a woman might have a weapon and know how to use it.'

Garwen walked on, Rhianna hurrying after her. The Romans would be making a big mistake if they believed Garwen was weak and helpless, she thought…

The storm broke over the Royal Place a little while later, the wind whistling round the Queen's House, rain lashing down on the thatch above their heads. It was the beginning of a cold, wet time, and the rain did not let up for several days. But Rhianna didn't mind. She loved being in the Queen's House, and so did her sister. Rhianna hadn't realised how bad living with Magunna had been for Eleri. Now she was almost like a different child – happy, playful, always following Maeve.

But then Rhianna had someone to look up to herself now too. She tried to be near Garwen as often as possible, so she could listen to her and ask more questions about the queen's body servants and what they did. Garwen didn't mind, and gave her straight answers, so Rhianna soon discovered that Garwen and the others believed in being strong and standing up for themselves – and not taking orders from men.

Rhianna also begged Garwen to teach her the skills she had talked about. It took a while, but eventually Garwen gave in and showed Rhianna a few ways to defend herself from an attack such as the one Segovax had tried. 'You should always use your enemy's own strength against him,' said Garwen. 'That fool Segovax couldn't believe I would be a threat, so he left himself open to the simplest of moves – a trip.' Rhianna worked hard with Garwen, who said she had some natural skill as a fighter. That was a very good moment – Rhianna felt ridiculously proud of Garwen's praise.

One evening Rhianna was sitting at the hearth with the queen and Garwen and a few more of the queen's body servants, all of them eating, talking and laughing.

'I see you have a new worshipper, Garwen,' said the queen after a while. 'Rhianna looks at you as if she thinks you might be a goddess. Should I be angry with her?'

Everyone stopped eating and fell silent, and Rhianna felt all their eyes upon her. She blushed, her cheeks burning, a slight tremor of fear running through her as well. The queen wasn't smiling and it was impossible to tell if she were joking or not.

'There is only one goddess, my lady, and I am not her,' Garwen said softly. 'She is the Morrigan, blessed be her name. No mortal woman could ever be compared to her, except perhaps you, our wonderful Queen Boudica, Heart of the Iceni…'

A murmur of agreement ran round the hearth. 'You flatter me, Garwen,' said the queen, smiling at last. 'But I could never be angry with Rhianna, even if she only has eyes for you at the moment, instead of her queen. I expect great things of her, and it is good to see her learning to be a true Iceni woman from you.'

The moment passed, their talk turning to lighter subjects. But that night as Rhianna lay wrapped in furs next to her sleeping sister, she thought again of what the queen had said. *Learning to be a true Iceni woman…* Rhianna was even gladder now that the queen had taken her in. She would much rather be a woman like the queen or Garwen than a screeching fool such as Magunna. And with that thought she fell asleep. Outside, the wind howled as if it were a creature from a nightmare.

Three days later Prasutagus died, and everything changed again.

* * *

It happened on the coldest winter day yet, one full moon after Rhianna and Eleri had moved into the Queen's House. The sky was iron-grey, and snowflakes danced in a cold wind from the east. One of the king's servants came running to the Queen's House, saying that he must speak with the queen. It seemed that the previous evening the king had felt unwell after eating his supper and had gone to his sleeping place early. A servant had gone to wake him in the morning and found him stiff and cold, a look of fear and agony on his face.

Rhianna was sitting by the hearth, mixing oats and goat's milk in a bowl for Eleri's morning meal, and heard everything. She saw the queen close her eyes, the way Rhianna knew she sometimes did when she was praying silently to the goddess, then she opened them once more and called for Garwen to come to her.

'Bring me my wolf-skin cloak, Garwen,' she said. 'It is cold outside and I must go to the King's House to make sure I am truly free from my husband at last…'

Things happened quickly after that. Rhianna went outside to see what was going on, taking Eleri with her. Word of the king's death had spread round the Royal Place at the speed of thought. A big crowd had gathered at the Meeting Ground, everyone murmuring, asking if it were true about the king, and trying to peer through the door of the King's House. Eventually the queen and Garwen emerged from within.

'What's happening, Boudica?' yelled a man Rhianna recognised. His name was Viducos and he was the most important noble in the Royal Place, a man all the other nobles listened to before they dared to speak. Viducos had many sons and large herds of horses and cattle, and he was tall and broad, his long, greying hair and moustaches still thick even though he was over forty summers old. His cloak was of the finest wool and clasped with a heavy gold brooch.

'There is not much to tell, Viducos,' said the queen without breaking stride. The crowd parted before her like the earth before the plough. 'Prasutagus is dead.'

Viducos stepped in front of her. Boudica stopped and frowned. Garwen made as if to move past her towards him, but the queen put out an arm to hold her back.

'I know,' said Viducos. 'I'm more interested in who will be our *next* king.'

'Why, Viducos, this is a surprise,' said the queen with a smile. 'Are you offering to be my husband? Whatever will your lovely wife Cara have to say about that?'

'You're welcome to him, my lady!' said a short, dumpy woman nearby.

The crowd laughed and jeered. 'Be quiet, Cara, this is serious!' said Viducos, scowling. 'The old king is dead, so now Boudica must choose a new one.'

'Is that so?' Boudica said, her smile fading. 'Perhaps I hated Prasutagus and only married him because you nobles and the Romans gave me no other choice. And perhaps now I will rule alone without a husband, as befits a true queen of the Iceni.'

Rhianna heard gasps of surprise, a woman calling out 'Heart of the Iceni!' others hushing each other. Silence fell and Rhianna thought it was as if the crowd was now a single beast, straining to listen.

Viducos stared at the queen, a puzzled look on his face. 'You can't be serious, Boudica…' he said. 'The queens of our tribe have always taken husbands. Besides, the Romans won't stand for you ruling alone.'

'He's right,' said another voice. 'They'll want to replace the king quickly.'

Rhianna turned and saw who had spoken. It was one of the king's bodyguards, a big, hard-looking man with a broken nose. His clothes were an odd mixture – his costly tunic and cloak were Roman, but were worn over plaid Iceni leggings. He was pushing roughly through the crowd, the rest of the bodyguards close behind him, shoving people out of their way. The man stopped in front of Viducos and the queen.

Boudica stared at him and the other bodyguards, her eyes glittering with hate.

'Tell me, people of the Royal Place of the Iceni!' she called out, the words ringing loud and clear across the Meeting Ground. 'Are you as tired of these dogs as I am? Are you tired of their yapping?' Rhianna thought that in her long grey wolf-skin cloak, and with her fiery hair streaming in the wind, she looked like a goddess.

'Yes, yes! We are!' the people yelled, their faces full of fury. Some of them shook their fists at the bodyguards, and the king's men began to look nervous, even fearful. They had weapons, swords and daggers in scabbards on their belts, but they were outnumbered at least twenty to one. They were vulnerable, and they knew it.

'Now just you hold on,' said the man with the broken nose. 'You can't...'

'Do not tell me what I can do,' hissed the queen. 'Your days of strutting around here are over. Perhaps I should let my people rip you to pieces.' There was more shouting, people agreeing with her, pushing and shoving the men. 'Or perhaps we should sacrifice you!' A great cheer went up. 'But I will let you go so you can take a message to your Roman masters. We are a free people – and I *will* rule alone!'

The bodyguards tried to leave, but the crowd surged forward and began to kick and punch them. 'I don't like it,' Eleri said quietly, moving in close to Rhianna. It *was* an ugly sight, Rhianna thought, hugging Eleri to her. Even some of the women and children joined in, although the bodyguards eventually broke away. Then Garwen and the queen's body servants stalked them like a pack of wolves, but with daggers in their hands, until the men finally escaped through the gates.

There was a great cheer as the bodyguards ran off down the track, heading southwards as fast as they could go. The crowd on the Meeting Ground started chanting: '*Long live the queen, Heart of the Iceni! Boudica! Boudica…*'

Rhianna suddenly felt a great wave of love for the queen too, and chanted along with the rest of the crowd. The bodyguards deserved to be chased from the Royal Place, she thought. Indeed, it could have been much worse for them – the only reason they were still alive was because of the queen's mercy. But Eleri remained silent and wide-eyed, and clung fearfully to Rhianna, gripping her hand even more tightly.

'It seems that the people have spoken,' said the queen, smiling at Viducos.

'So they have,' said Viducos, shrugging and smiling back at her. 'I'm impressed, Boudica. But we both know it isn't as simple as that. And I'm sure the other nobles will agree. You and I need to talk.'

'Not now, Viducos,' said Boudica, turning away. 'This is a day of celebration for me, and for the tribe. Come, Rhianna, we should get your sister out of the cold…'

It was a good day in the Queen's House, with singing and feasting and fun, and so were the next five days. Rhianna had never seen the queen looking so happy. It was as if a shadow had been lifted from her and everyone else in the Royal Place.

But on the seventh day the Romans came.

CHAPTER FOUR
Red-Crested Helmets

T he day started with a visit to the Queen's House from Viducos and several more great men of the tribe. They had come twice before to speak with the queen and both times she had sent them away. Today, however, she graciously allowed them in and let them sit around her hearth. Garwen quietly told everyone else to go outside.

'What is happening, Garwen?' Rhianna asked her. 'Why are they here?'

'To tell the queen they want her to get married again, of course,' said Garwen. 'They still don't seem to realise that the time for kings is over, that we have returned to the rule of women and the goddess. But don't worry, they will before long…'

Rhianna decided to take Eleri to the horse corrals down by the gate. It was her sister's favourite place and she would be happy there until they could return to the Queen's House. As they walked though the Royal Place, Rhianna thought about Garwen's words – and hoped she was right. But Viducos and the others had looked sullen and ready to argue, and it seemed as if the Royal Place crackled with tension.

There was a dusting of snow on the ground and a sharp wind, although this time Rhianna had remembered Eleri's warm cloak, and her own. The Iceni had famously always been a horse-loving tribe, and in summer the Royal Place's corrals were full of horses, each branded with an owner's mark. In winter the animals were kept inside, in thatched stables, and when Rhianna and Eleri arrived there the corrals were almost empty. Only two horses were being exercised, a fine pair of young chestnut stallions.

Rhianna had also remembered to bring some stale crusts of bread. Eleri fed the horses through the rough-split logs of the fence, laughing as the beasts nuzzled at her hands with their soft mouths. 'Easy there,' said a boy who was inside the corral. Rhianna recognised him as Gwydion, a young son of Viducos, and realised that the horses must be his father's chariot team. Viducos was very proud of them.

Suddenly both horses looked up, ears pricked as if they could hear something. Rhianna heard it too, a steady *THUMP-THUMP-THUMP*, and soon she could feel it as well – the ground was trembling beneath her feet. The sound seemed to be coming from outside the Royal Place and Rhianna turned to look at the gate, which was open, as it usually was these days. And then suddenly a column of armed men came marching through it, four abreast, their iron-shod boots rising and falling together.

Rhianna knew instantly they were Roman soldiers – she had never seen one before, but she had heard descriptions of them. They wore blood-red tunics and leggings, and armour made of overlapping strips of metal. Their iron helmets were round and plain, with wide cheek-pieces on either side, although some of the soldiers had helmets topped by bristling crests of horse hair dyed bright scarlet. Each man had a short sword and a dagger on his belt, and a long curved shield slung on his back.

They were a terrifying sight, and Rhianna pulled Eleri closer to her. Others stood watching, their faces full of fear. Rhianna saw mothers grab their children and run into their houses, and a couple of young boys dashing off towards the upper part of the Royal Place. A group of men on horses brought up the rear of the column. Their armour was richer; their chests were covered in breastplates that gleamed in the bright winter sun and cloaks draped over the hindquarters of their horses.

One of the horsemen was not dressed as a soldier, but wore a thick bearskin cloak over a white tunic. His dark hair was cropped close to his skull and his nose was like a hawk's beak. As he rode past on a huge black horse, he turned to stare down at Rhianna and Eleri, his eyes cold and hard...

Rhianna was suddenly desperate for the protection of the queen and Garwen, and hurried Eleri away. She decided it was best to avoid the track the Romans were using, but that meant going the long way round. By the time they arrived at the Meeting Ground, the Romans were already there. The column had halted and was dividing, several hundred soldiers fanning out, those with red-crested helmets yelling orders. Rhianna dashed through the lines of soldiers with Eleri, and up to the doors of the Queen's House.

At that moment the queen emerged, Garwen on one side of her, Viducos on the other. Behind them were Tegan and Maeve, the rest of the queen's body servants, and the men who had come with Viducos. Rhianna took Eleri over to Garwen, who put her strong arms round them both. For a brief instant Rhianna didn't feel quite so scared, but then she looked up and her stomach churned with fear.

A line of Romans faced them, each soldier now holding his shield on his left arm. Another line stood fifty paces behind them, although they were facing in the opposite direction, towards the lower part of the Royal Place. They too held their shields, and a crowd of the Royal Place's people had gathered beyond them. Rhianna could hear people calling out, although most were clearly nervous and kept a safe distance.

The horsemen had paused between the lines, but they slowly advanced once more, the soldiers in front of the Queen's House parting to let them through. They stopped a short distance in front of the doors, the man with the cold, hard eyes staring down at Boudica. She proudly returned his gaze and a tense stillness fell across the Meeting Ground, the only sound that of the man's horse briefly snickering.

'I bid you welcome to my Royal Place, Roman,' said the queen at last. 'We Iceni are known for our hospitality to those who come to our lands in peace.'

'So you are Boudica then, widow of King Prasutagus?' said the hard-eyed man. To Rhianna's surprise he spoke in their tongue, or at least something like it, his accent mangling the words. 'The woman who now calls herself Queen of the Iceni?'

'She *IS* our queen!' Garwen hissed. 'Be careful how you speak to her, Roman!'

'I will speak to her in any way I choose,' said the man. 'I am Publius Catus Decianus, procurator of the Province of Britannia. I have come here in the name of His Imperial Majesty Nero to inform you that the lands of the Iceni are to be taken into his empire, and that from this day forward you will all be his subjects.'

'What are you talking about?' spluttered Viducos. 'We have an agreement! We are allowed to rule ourselves so long as we pay your tribute and obey your rules!'

'Quite right,' Decianus said softly. He smiled and Rhianna felt her blood turn cold. There was something very cruel about this Roman. 'But you have broken our rules, have you not? The king's

46

bodyguards told us that his widow had openly declared she was going to rule alone, and Rome cannot allow that.'

'Those men are nothing but scum,' said Boudica. 'I should have killed them.'

'It would have made no difference,' said Decianus. 'Do you really think they are the only spies we have here? You cannot escape the eyes and ears of the Roman Empire. We know everything that happens among you filthy savages.'

'You Romans are the savages, not us,' said the queen. 'This is our land, and…'

'Be quiet, woman!' said Decianus. 'The time for talking is over.' He turned to the soldiers behind him and snapped an order in Latin. Several of the men swiftly moved forward to seize the queen and her daughters, dragging them away from the Queen's House and from the others standing behind her. Tegan and Maeve screamed, and Garwen attacked one of the soldiers, punching his back and kicking his legs.

Several more of the queen's body servants followed her, shoving past Rhianna in their

47

fury, almost knocking Eleri over. Rhianna just managed to hold on to her sister, then watched horrified as the rest of the soldiers behind Decianus drew their swords, the sharp blades glinting in the weak winter sunlight.

'Leave them be, Garwen!' the queen called out. 'They are too many, and they will slaughter you and the others!'

'Wise words, Boudica,' said Decianus, looking down at her. 'There is no need for anyone to die today. But of course, you must be punished for your presumption. I therefore decree fifty lashes each for your daughters, and a hundred for you.'

'No! Tegan! Maeve!' Boudica screamed, but the soldiers had already forced both girls on to their knees. Their gowns were roughly stripped from their backs, and a Roman soldier behind them suddenly produced a long leather horsewhip.

Rhianna turned away and put her hands over Eleri's eyes. Yet there was no escaping the sound of the whip whistling through the air and striking flesh, or the screams of Tegan and Maeve. Soon Rhianna felt she could bear it no more.

But she still had to stand there and listen.

* * *

After the beatings, Decianus allowed Garwen and the other servants to take Boudica and her daughters into the Queen's House to tend their wounds. Rhianna followed with Eleri, trying not to stare at the terrible gashes which covered their backs. Tegan and Maeve had passed out while they were being beaten, but Boudica was still conscious and more worried about her daughters than herself.

'Hush, my lady: I will take care of them, and of you,' Garwen said softly as she knelt beside the queen. They had laid Boudica and her daughters face down on rugs beside the hearth. 'Fetch water and clean cloths! We must try to stop the bleeding.'

'Will they live?' said Viducos, who had come into the Queen's House as well. 'I have seen strong men die after fewer strokes of the lash than they've had…'

'That is because men are weaklings,' said Garwen, glaring at him. 'The queen is stronger

49

than any man, as are her daughters. And we will pray to the goddess.'

Viducos frowned, opening his mouth to say something else, but just then somebody called his name. The men he had been with were standing by the door, peering out. There was more noise coming from the Meeting Ground, Romans yelling in Latin, Iceni voices shouting in reply. Rhianna couldn't make out what they were all saying and she didn't want to know. But Viducos clearly did, and he soon left with the other nobles.

'Will... will Maeve really be all right?' said Eleri, her voice little more than a whisper. There were tears on her cheeks and a heartbreaking look of sorrow on her face. Rhianna felt guilty – she should have realised how upset Eleri would be. The bond between Eleri and Maeve had grown even stronger as the winter went on.

'I'm sure she will,' said Garwen, reaching over to give Eleri's hand a squeeze.

'Could Eleri help in some way?' said Rhianna. 'I'm sure she would like to.'

'Good idea,' said Garwen, smiling. 'There will be lots you can do, Eleri…'

They cared for Boudica and her daughters through the day. Garwen managed to stop the bleeding, and she put a special healing salve on their backs, one she said that Boudica herself had made. There were reports from time to time about what was happening outside. The Romans were still in the Royal Place, stealing whatever they could find in the houses, beating anyone who argued with them or got in their way. Rhianna heard people begging for mercy and screams of fear and pain, and the voices of Romans shouting in Latin, and sometimes brokenly in the tongue of the Iceni.

It wasn't until the afternoon that the Romans left, marching out of the Royal Place with five wagons that they had taken, each of them loaded with loot. They took a hundred horses too, including the chestnut stallions belonging to Viducos. Decianus had said the extra 'tribute' was part of Rome's 'punishment' for what their queen had done.

Hatred for the Romans filled Rhianna's heart, but she was frightened as well. Some people said they would come back, that there would always be Roman soldiers in the Royal Place from now on, that they would build a fort as they had elsewhere...

But then Boudica rose from her bed, and the world changed again.

CHAPTER FIVE

The Queen's Bidding

Three days went past before the queen and her daughters began to recover, and Rhianna was sure Garwen didn't sleep during that time. Whenever Rhianna went to see how she could help, Garwen was at their side, holding their heads up to give them cow's milk mixed with honey to drink, or one of Boudica's own healing potions. She checked on their wounds, and put more salve on them with her gentle touch.

Then one evening the queen pushed away the cup Garwen was holding to her lips. Rhianna was there with Eleri, and Tegan and Maeve were sitting up, eating stew from bowls. Fragrant logs burned in the hearth, and the cold wind moaned outside.

'Enough, Garwen,' said the queen, her voice husky. 'Is Rhianna here?'

'Yes, my lady, I am,' said Rhianna, stepping out of the shadows.

'Good,' said the queen. She reached up from where she lay beside the hearth and took Rhianna's hand. 'I must beg your forgiveness, Rhianna. I promised that you and your sister would be safe in my care. Yet it was my fault the Romans came.'

'But... but we have nothing to forgive you for!' said Rhianna. 'You and Tegan and Maeve are the ones who have suffered. The Romans didn't hurt Eleri or me.'

'I am glad of that,' said the queen. She pushed herself into a sitting position and winced with pain. 'Yet none of us will be safe so long as the Romans hold power anywhere in Britannia.

I know this because the goddess came to me in my dreams while I was sleeping, and she told me so. She also told me what I should do.'

Boudica now rose to her feet and stood there swaying, her face pale in the firelight. Garwen gasped and rushed to her side, but the queen pushed her away again.

'No, I must stand on my own feet,' she said. 'And so must my daughters.'

Tegan and Maeve put down their bowls and slowly stood too. Their young faces were as pale and drawn and tired as their mother's, and Rhianna felt a surge of pity for them. All three were wearing simple night shifts that were stained with their blood and crumpled from three days and nights of pain and restlessness.

'Summon the tribe, Garwen,' said the queen. 'I must speak to my people.'

'But it is dark, my lady,' Garwen murmured. 'The sun has long since set.'

'DO AS I SAY, GARWEN!' the queen shouted, startling Rhianna. She had never heard the queen raise her voice. Soon Garwen and the

other body servants were running through the Royal Place, telling everyone to gather at the Meeting Ground.

A short while later, Rhianna was standing outside the Queen's House, holding Eleri's hand and looking at the crowd. It seemed that every man, woman and child in the Royal Place had come at the queen's bidding. They waited silently, many of them holding high the torches they had brought to light their way. The sky was a deep black, with only a few stars visible, and a bitter wind blew from the west.

Garwen stood beside Rhianna and Eleri, the other servants behind them. At last the doors of the Queen's House opened and Boudica emerged, Tegan and Maeve on either side of her. They still wore their night shifts – the queen had refused to allow Garwen to bring them clean gowns of the kind they usually wore in public. A groan went up from the crowd when they saw Boudica and her daughters. But there were cheers too, and voices calling out: *'Queen Boudica! Heart of the Iceni!'*

She waited a moment, then held up her hand. The crowd quickly fell silent.

'You all know what was done to my daughters, and to me,' she said, her voice ringing out. 'The Romans brought shame on us, here in my Royal Place. But at least now I know what we should do – what we should have done long ago!'

'Tell us, Boudica!' a man yelled from the crowd, and several others shouted the same. Rhianna felt something important was about to happen and sensed a sudden wave of real excitement in the crowd. Eleri gripped her hand tightly.

'We will bring shame on the Romans in return!' the queen said, and the crowd cheered. 'We will rise against them!' she said, and the cheering grew louder. 'We will sweep them from our lands in blood and fire – and take back our freedom!'

Now the crowd roared and somebody yelled, 'DEATH TO THE ROMANS!' Others took up the cry and Rhianna joined in, all the horror and hate and fear pouring out of her in those words: *'DEATH TO THE ROMANS! DEATH TO THE ROMANS!'*

The queen smiled and the chanting went on for a long time. Rhianna noticed Viducos in the front rank of the crowd, standing there with his arms crossed.

He wasn't chanting, and he wasn't smiling either.

* * *

Viducos confronted the queen early the next morning. He came into the Queen's House and refused to leave until she listened to him. Everyone else was there – Garwen, Tegan and Maeve, Rhianna and Eleri – but he clearly didn't care.

'I've been speaking to the other nobles. We think it's madness to rebel against the Romans, Boudica,' he said. 'They're too powerful. They have conquered almost the whole world and few have been able to stand against them. Caradoc of the Catuvellauni tried, and they crushed him.'

Rhianna knew the story of Caradoc, or Caratacus as the Romans called him. The territory of the Catuvellauni was south-west of the Iceni

58

lands. They had been the strongest tribe in Britannia, yet the Romans defeated them. Their chief Caradoc fought on, but Queen Cartimandua of the Brigantes betrayed him to the Romans. They took him in chains to Rome, and his people became subjects of the Roman Empire.

'So what would you men have us do, Viducos?' said the queen. 'You want me to give in to the Romans without a fight? I would rather die than live as a slave of their evil empire! And do you not want vengeance for what they did to your son?'

Gwydion had tried to stop the Romans taking his father's horses and they had beaten him badly. The boy had not woken since, and was not expected to live much longer. Rhianna could see on his face how the queen's words brought pain to Viducos.

'Yes, I do,' he said. 'But we are not ready for war. We have few weapons, and besides, the men have forgotten how to use them. It's been many years since the tribe took to the war-trail. We'll need allies too. We can't fight the Romans on our own.'

'All of that can be solved,' said the queen. 'Let's work out how…'

The queen drew Viducos apart, talking to him all the time. Rhianna watched, fascinated, and Garwen smiled. 'Viducos is doomed,' she said. 'Mark my words, Rhianna, before this day's end he will be happy to do the queen's bidding.'

Garwen was right – Viducos was soon organising the men, persuading them to reveal the special hiding places for their weapons. It turned out there were more than he had thought – old swords, spears, helmets and shields that belonged to men who had once been warriors. Over the next few days Rhianna got used to the sight of men training with weapons, the older men showing the younger ones what to do.

She also got used to seeing Garwen and the queen's body servants training with weapons. Rhianna had no idea where they'd got them – Garwen simply emerged one day from the Queen's House ready for war. Now she wore a plain tunic and plaid leggings, and she had a fine sword in a scabbard on her belt. She also carried a spear and a long shield, its entire front covered in a pattern of swirling lines like flowing water. The others came out behind her and they were all armed too.

'What in the name of the gods are you doing?' said a surprised Viducos. He was training some men at the Meeting Place. 'War is only for men, not girls!'

'I don't think so, Viducos,' said Garwen, smiling. Rhianna was watching from the doorway of the Queen's House and Garwen winked at her. 'In fact, how about putting it to the test?' Garwen continued. 'I'll take on any of you right now.'

Viducos spluttered, saying he didn't want to hurt her, but some of the men laughed and jeered at him, asking if he was too scared to fight a girl. Rhianna saw that one of the men was Segovax. He stayed silent, his cold, mean eyes fixed on Garwen.

'Very well,' said Viducos, sighing. 'I'll just have to teach you a lesson.'

Garwen grinned, handed her spear to one of her companions, drew her sword – and advanced swiftly on Viducos. It was over before he even knew it had begun. Garwen moved like a wolf, light on her feet and full of menace, and beat his shield down with her sword before tripping him. He crashed heavily to the ground, just as Segovax had done, and she stood over him, her sword point at his throat.

'You boys clearly need to train a lot harder, Viducos,' she said. Then she raised her sword and helped him to his feet. 'The Romans won't be as merciful as me…'

* * *

Time passed, the winter deepened, and as usual the people of the Royal Place gathered at the Meeting Ground to mark the longest night of the year. They built a huge fire that lit up the sky, and made sacrifices to the gods so they would let the sun start to grow strong again, and the days become longer. Everybody ate and drank and danced, but Rhianna sensed there was an edge of worry to the celebration. She felt very anxious herself and sought out Garwen so she could talk to her.

'Why have the Romans not come back, Garwen?' she asked. They were standing at the side of the Meeting Ground, watching people dance round the fire – young couples, mothers with their children, the old. Rhianna saw Magunna drinking and laughing. 'Everyone said Decianus would send soldiers to hold the Royal Place.'

'He won't do it until the weather is better,' said Garwen. 'For now he will keep his soldiers in their forts. It will be easier in the spring to march across country.'

Rhianna knew there was truth in her words. The hardest part of the winter was yet to come, and it would be madness to travel far when there might be snow.

'Do you really think we can beat them?' said Rhianna. 'It seems impossible.'

'They are not gods,' said Garwen. 'They are mortal like us, and that means we can kill them if we fight well. Remember, we will have the goddess on our side.'

'But only if we are worthy, and serve her as we should,' said the queen, who had silently come up behind them. Rhianna was startled, and turned to her. Boudica looked strange and scary in her wolf-skin cloak, half her face in deep shadow, the other half lit by the leaping red flames of the fire. 'Yet I am sure you know that, Rhianna.'

'I do, my lady,' said Rhianna, remembering her mother's words. 'The goddess demands prayers and devotion – we must worship her with all our hearts.'

'The goddess also demands blood,' said the queen, her expression grim, her voice suddenly dark and full of menace. 'The tribe has not fed her properly for many years, but that is about to change. We will need to make many sacrifices to her…'

Garwen bowed to her, but Rhianna felt confused. Her mother had said the goddess could be angry, especially when people who worshipped her were treated cruelly. Yet she had also said the goddess was kind and loving, and took care of the weak. Now it was as if the queen were talking of a different goddess… But Rhianna told herself she had no right to question the queen, and bowed too.

Later, the queen gave an order for a great stone to be brought to the Meeting Ground and set up as an altar. She told Garwen to have seven sheep fetched from her personal flock, and sacrificed them herself. A crowd gathered to watch as two men hauled the first squealing, bucking beast on to the altar and the queen cut its throat with a bronze dagger, hot blood splashing across the rough surface of the rock.

'These lives I give to you, Goddess!' she said. 'You who are three in one – the girl, the mother and the crone – you who created all gods and stand for all women. And this I promise, Goddess – we will give you more lives, much more blood…'

Rhianna watched as the queen prepared to kill the second sheep. It fought hard, spooked by the smell of blood, its dark brown eyes rolling with terror.

Eyes that looked just like Eleri's, Rhianna thought with a shiver.

CHAPTER SIX

Drums of War

I n early spring, when the days grew longer and warmer, the warriors began to train in their chariots. Most tribes in Britannia had used such things before the Romans came. They were made of ash wood, had wicker sides and handrails, large, iron-hooped, spoked wheels, and a long pole at the front with a pair of horses harnessed to it. Each chariot carried a driver to hold the reins and a warrior to fight. In battle, the chariots charged the enemy and were followed by warriors who fought on foot.

The chariot training ground was the same as the racing course at the Summer Gathering, the flat land by the river. Many people went to watch the spectacle, but Rhianna thought it would bring back bad memories, so she kept Eleri away. Besides, Eleri was already feeling unhappy. Maeve was struggling with what the Romans had done to her, and she spent most days sitting by the hearth, ignoring everyone – including Eleri. It broke Rhianna's heart to see how that made her little sister suffer.

Rhianna's life was dominated by the queen. Boudica had begun to expect Rhianna to be with her constantly through the day, to help her dress in the morning, to bring her meals, and to perform other tasks she might set her. Rhianna knew it was a great honour, and it brought another advantage – she was with the queen whenever she talked to Garwen and Viducos, so she found out much that was interesting.

The queen had clearly listened to Viducos and agreed with him that the Iceni would need allies in the fight against the Romans. She sent messengers to the chiefs of the two neighbouring tribes, Andorix of the Catuvellauni and Cumenal of the Trinovantes, inviting them to the Royal Place for a Great Council.

They came on a bright, cool day, each chief riding in with a small band of warriors. The queen welcomed them warmly and soon both men were sitting beside her hearth. Viducos and Garwen were there too, sitting on either side of the queen. Rhianna sat behind her and studied the two chiefs. Andorix was tall and lean, his hair and beard the colour of a fox's pelt. Cumenal was a bear of a man, his tunic tight over his broad shoulders and chest, his hair and beard thick and black and bushy. The queen spoke to them lightly at first, asking if their families were well and their journeys had been good. They stared at her with stony faces and gave very short answers.

'Enough chatter, Boudica,' Cumenal growled at last. 'We know why you have summoned us here. You want us to join in your war against the Romans.'

'You are well informed, Cumenal,' said the queen, frowning. 'Does that mean you have spies in my Royal Place too? I thought only the Romans did such things.'

'We know what happened to you and your daughters, and what you are planning,' said Andorix, shrugging. 'The question is whether you will succeed or not.'

The queen smiled. 'I will lead my people to victory,' she replied. 'Is it not already in my name?' Rhianna hadn't thought about it, but now she realised what the queen said was true – the name Boudica came from the Iceni word for 'victory in battle'. 'But together we will be strong enough to defeat the Romans quickly,' the queen was saying, 'and clear them from Britannia forever.'

'I'm not sure you can do that,' said Cumenal. 'They are very hard to beat.'

'So why have you come then?' said the queen. 'I will tell you. Your people hate the Romans as much as we do…'

Garwen had told Rhianna what had happened to the Trinovantes. The Romans had taken their Royal Place, a great settlement named Camulodunum, in honour of the tribe's main god, Camulos. They had turned it into a Roman city and, when the Roman Emperor Claudius died, they had built a huge temple to Claudius at the city's heart. This seemed strange to Rhianna. They executed many who had fought against them, and made many more into slaves. Then the land round the city was given to Roman soldiers too old to fight any more, and they settled there with their families.

'We have good reason to hate the Romans,' said Andorix. 'I am the son of Adminios, who was brother to Caradoc, the great chief we of the Catuvellauni have never forgotten. The Romans killed or enslaved many of our people, and like the Trinovantes we live in their shadow. So we seek revenge against them, just like you. And we came because it seems that this might be the right moment to rebel for all of us.'

'Is that so?' said the queen. She leaned forward, her eyes fixed on him…

Andorix laid out his thoughts for her. Rhianna had heard some of it from Garwen, but much was new. It seemed that Decianus was not the most powerful Roman in Britannia any more. He had to obey the new governor, Gaius Suetonius Paulinus, a general who had commanded armies all over the Empire. But Emperor Nero had given Paulinus a special mission – he was to conquer the rest of Britannia.

Paulinus had plenty of soldiers for the task. The Romans divided their army into enormous war-bands of five thousand men, which they called 'legions', and there were four in Britannia. One was in the far west, in the lands of the Dumnonii, and one was in the south, near the city of Londinium that the Romans had founded on the banks of the great River Tamesis. The other two were in the north, watching the Brigantes.

'But my spies in Londinium tell me Paulinus plans to bring most of the legions together for a summer campaign in the north-west,' said

Andorix. 'He thinks that if he can break the power of the Druids, the rest of Britannia will fall to him…'

Rhianna knew that the high priests of the Druids had a sacred place in the far north-west, an island called Mona. Druids from all over Britannia went there to learn spells and sorcery, and to make sacrifices to gods such as Lugh and Cernunnos. That meant they had influence in many tribes, and the Romans saw them as a threat.

'Ah, so this summer is the *perfect* time to rebel…' said the queen.

Andorix and Cumenal looked at each other, then turned to the queen and nodded. Thus it was agreed that the three tribes would rise together against the Romans.

Rhianna felt thrilled and terrified all at the same time.

* * *

Two moons later the Iceni were ready to take to the war-trail. The warriors were trained, and most carried weapons of reasonable quality – the Royal Place's smiths had made as many swords and spears as they could. Food had been gathered and loaded on wagons, although the queen said they didn't need to take much as they would defeat the Romans before harvest time. A day had been set to join with the allies.

The people of the outlying settlements gathered at the Royal Place as well, their tents and campfires filling the fields around as far as Rhianna could see. Whole families came, the old and young, men, women and their children.

'I don't understand, Garwen,' Rhianna said, looking at them from the fighting platform on the stockade. 'Won't many of these people just get in your way?'

'In a battle, the warriors will be at the front, facing the enemy, and everyone else will be at the rear,' said Garwen. 'Besides, what if the Romans decide to try an attack on the tribe while we are on the war-trail? Those we leave behind would have no protection. Yet there is a secret, safe place in the marshes where a few people will be staying. I'm sure the queen would send Eleri there if you were to ask her.'

Rhianna would be going on the war-trail with the queen, and she had been worrying about Eleri. Should she take her little sister with her? There was definitely danger ahead, and for a brief instant Rhianna felt tempted to speak to the queen and send Eleri to the safe place. But Rhianna didn't like the idea of being apart from Eleri and she saw the sense in what Garwen had said about protection.

'Eleri will come with me,' said Rhianna, and so that was settled too.

Two days later, on a bright, warm morning, the tribe set off southward, Boudica leading her people. She rode in a chariot drawn by a pair of white horses, the finest in all the Iceni herds, with Garwen standing beside her as the driver. They were followed by ten chariots bearing the queen's other body servants, and behind them came another hundred, driven by Viducos and the best of the men he had trained.

Next was a line of big ox-drawn wagons piled high with sacks and baskets of food, spare weapons and tents, each driven by one of the warriors. Rhianna and Eleri sat behind the driver in the queen's wagon, which followed the chariots. It was packed with everything the queen thought she might need while she was away from the Royal Place. Eleri chattered as if this were some kind of summer outing. Rhianna was excited, but there was much fear in her heart as well.

'I've never seen so many people!' Eleri said. The rest of the tribe walked behind the wagons, thousands of men, women and children. Most of the men and some of the women carried spears or clubs or other makeshift weapons, and many seemed as excited as Eleri. Rhianna tried to count them, but she soon gave up and concentrated on looking ahead, keeping her eyes on the queen and Garwen in the distance.

They travelled for three days and made camp each evening. The queen had a huge tent, bigger than a house, and gave Rhianna and Eleri a small one of their own. At dusk on the fourth day they came to the river that divided the Iceni lands from those of the Trinovantes. Beyond it lay a vast camp. Rhianna could see chariots and wagons, tents and shelters, people and dogs and lines of tethered horses, and campfires glowing everywhere. The allies were waiting, as had been agreed.

Andorix and Cumenal rode out to greet the queen, splashing over the river on their horses. They said there was room for the Iceni, so the queen ordered the tribe to make camp, adding their wagons to the protective circle around them all.

That night a great feast was held. Sheep were roasted, fat hissing as it dripped into the red flames of the cooking fires, and people dipped their cups into big bowls of foaming barley beer. Rhianna and Eleri sat behind the queen, alongside Garwen, Tegan and Maeve. Viducos, Andorix and Cumenal were nearby with their families. A huge crowd stood around the open space before them, another fire burning in the middle, the logs almost white-hot. Suddenly seven black-robed men started beating giant drums. The thunderous sound made Rhianna's body throb and her teeth ache.

'Druids!' Garwen yelled, grinning. 'They're playing the drums of war!'

Rhianna looked at the men with more interest now, but was soon distracted. A group of young warriors from all three tribes started a war dance. They carried spears and were stripped to the waist to reveal new tattoos, swirling lines that were raw beneath the blueness, and their faces were covered in streaks of warpaint the colour of blood.

They stamped and whirled and leaped through the fire, screaming their war cries.

Garwen turned to Rhianna and rolled her eyes. 'We do it better,' she yelled in Rhianna's ear. 'I've a mind to show them just how much better, in fact…'

She didn't get the chance. Suddenly the drumming and dancing stopped, and the crowd cheered and whistled. Then the queen rose to her feet and they fell silent. For a moment the only sound in the camp was the crackling of the fire's flames.

'People of the tribes!' the queen called out at last, her voice ringing in the still night air. 'We have not always been friends – we have often fought each other in the past. But now we have joined together to fight the Romans. They came to take our freedom, and we have suffered under them for too long. I know many of you are not used to being led by a woman. Yet will you follow me against our enemy?'

'We will!' the crowd roared, the Catuvellauni and the Trinovantes as well as the Iceni. Rhianna saw Viducos exchange a look and a shrug with Andorix and Cumenal. Garwen noticed it too, and shook her head as if to say 'Men! They're hopeless…'

'I am glad to hear it!' said the queen, laughing, the firelight glinting in her eyes. 'Enjoy yourselves tonight, then sleep well. The killing begins tomorrow!'

The crowd roared even more loudly. Rhianna thought it sounded like a great beast hungry for blood, and shivered. She looked round the circle of eager faces and thought that with their mouths open and eyes wide they all looked the same.

Suddenly her gaze snagged on one face, a woman staring back at her. Rhianna realised it was Magunna, and beside her was Segovax, baying with the rest.

Then the shadows shifted and she could see them no more.

CHAPTER SEVEN

A Great Victory

The tribes broke camp and moved on the next morning, Rhianna and Eleri in the wagon as before. There were three times as many chariots, warriors and wagons now, and the crowd that formed most of the column was enormous, a horde of people kicking up a great cloud of dust as they walked. They had seen no rain for a while, the sun had been shining in a blue sky for days, and the ground was dry as the bones of the dead.

Around noon a rider came galloping up from the rear, a scout by the look of him, Rhianna thought. His horse was panting, foam flying from its mouth. Garwen had told her they always kept scouts in front and behind the column, and on the flanks too, so the Romans couldn't surprise them. This scout was clearly in a hurry and suddenly Rhianna's stomach flipped over when she thought what that might mean.

The scout roughly reined in his horse beside the queen's chariot. He spoke to her, pointing in the direction from which he had come. Even at some distance, Rhianna could tell he was excited. The queen listened intently, her face serious, and soon gave an order for the column to halt. Then Viducos ordered the wagons and people to move out of the way so the chariots could turn round and head for the rear.

They came thundering down the track, Garwen and the queen leading. Rhianna waved and called out, and she could see the queen telling Garwen to stop.

'There are some Roman soldiers behind us, Rhianna,' said the queen, smiling at her. 'Would you like to come and watch the warriors deal with them? Don't worry about Eleri. I'm sure she can look after herself while you're with me… '

Rhianna was briefly unsure, and surprised the queen should talk about Eleri in that way. But there was clearly no arguing with her.

Moments later Rhianna was standing in the speeding chariot, gripping the front rail, the queen holding her. Garwen stood beside them, the reins in her hands, urging on the horses, as their hooves pounded along the track. Rhianna had never known anything so thrilling, and Garwen grinned to see her laughing at the sheer joy of it. After a time the track rose up a short slope, taking them through some trees and out to the edge of a wide valley. They halted there, and the rest of the chariots fanned out on either side of them.

Rhianna looked down and saw a line of Roman soldiers marching four abreast through the valley, their red crests and metal armour bright in the sun. Leading them was a small group of men on horseback. The one right at the front was wearing a helmet with a tall white crest. He must be their leader, Rhianna thought. Another, bigger group of soldiers on horseback brought up the rear. Garwen had told her the Romans had a special name for their mounted soldiers – they called them the cavalry.

Viducos jumped down from his chariot and ran over to the queen. 'We think it's one of the northern legions, probably the Ninth,' he said. 'Not the whole legion, mind you – it looks like there's only fifteen hundred foot soldiers, with maybe five hundred cavalry at the most. They've marched pretty hard and fast too. Andorix says his spies told him they were still in their fort at Lindum only seven days ago.'

'So they will be tired,' said the queen. 'And we clearly outnumber them.'

'Oh, by a long way,' said Viducos, his face grim. He looked beyond her and Rhianna turned round. The foot-warriors were arriving, a great mass of men walking out of the trees and gathering behind the chariots. Many had stripped to the waist to show off their tattoos and had daubed warpaint on their faces. Rhianna thought they looked keen to fight, like hunting hounds waiting impatiently to be unleashed.

'Well then, what are you waiting for?' said the queen, smiling back at him. 'Just get on with it, will you? Come, Rhianna, we shall watch the battle from here…'

The queen stepped off the chariot, and Rhianna followed her. Half a dozen body servants stayed as guards for the queen, and Viducos ran back to his own chariot. Soon there were shouts and whistling and horses neighing all along the line as it began to move forward, slowly at first, but soon gathering speed. The Romans halted and some pointed up the slope, but they had little time to prepare. Garwen led the charge down to the Roman column – and the chariots crashed through it.

Rhianna had never seen a battle before, so she had no idea what to expect. In fact it was difficult to see much from where she was standing, especially after the warriors on foot caught up with the chariots. It just seemed to be a crowd of men pushing and shoving, blades rising and falling, chariots wheeling round to charge once more. Rhianna worried about Garwen, but she couldn't even get a glimpse of her. The noise was terrific – the yelling, the clashing of metal, the screams of men in pain.

Suddenly the Roman cavalry turned and fled as fast as they could ride. Before long it was clear the battle was over and that the Romans had lost. A single chariot came back up the slope and Rhianna's heart leaped when she saw it was Garwen.

Garwen stopped the chariot in front of the queen and Rhianna, the horses snorting and shaking their heads. 'My lady, victory is ours,' she said, her voice unsteady. Her face was pale and covered in a sheen of sweat. Rhianna was shocked to see how quickly she had changed in the short time since she had charged down the slope. 'The warriors are calling for you,' Garwen went on. 'Let me take you to them.'

'Of course!' said the queen, and she climbed into the chariot again. Rhianna didn't move. She wasn't sure she wanted to go down to the battlefield. But the queen gave her a questioning look and held out a hand, so Rhianna stepped up beside her.

Garwen drove the chariot slowly back down the slope. At first all Rhianna could see was a crowd of warriors. They made way for the chariot, their faces happy as they looked up at the queen. 'Boudica!' they yelled, raising their swords and spears to her in triumph.

'The Romans fell before us like wheat before the scythe,' a young man called out. 'We have taken vengeance for what they did to you, Boudica!'

'You have done well!' Boudica replied. 'But we have not taken enough vengeance yet! More blood will have to flow before the goddess is truly satisfied...'

The warriors roared, and banged swords and spears against their shields. A moment later the chariot emerged from the crowd and into the flat bottom of the valley. There were bodies everywhere, mostly Roman, but quite a few men from the tribes too. Rhianna felt her stomach twist into knots, and she tried hard not to look too closely.

They stopped at last in an open space that had been cleared of bodies. A group of Romans was there, perhaps fifty men kneeling with their heads bowed and hands tied behind their backs. Rhianna realised they must be the only survivors of the Roman force, and marvelled at how many men must have died. Warriors stood around, jabbing at the men with spears and swords, and laughing when they flinched. Viducos was nearby, watching from his chariot, his face a mask of fury.

'Don't kill *all* the prisoners, Viducos,' said the queen. 'I am going to need them.'

She asked if they had killed the Roman general who had been leading the column, and Viducos replied that he seemed to have escaped with the cavalry. But Rhianna was no longer listening. She felt hot and cold at the same time, her skin was clammy, her head was spinning and her stomach was twisting painfully.

'Rhianna, are you all right?' said Garwen, putting a hand on her shoulder.

It was too late. Rhianna was just able to lean out of the chariot…

Then she was sick until her stomach was empty.

* * *

They made camp that night further up the valley from the battlefield and had a feast to celebrate. There was eating and drinking and more drumming, and warriors capering around the fire in Roman helmets and armour, trampling on the Roman standards, the poles topped with a figure of an eagle that the legions carried with them into battle. The prisoners sat silently, heads bowed, people taunting them.

Rhianna sat with Eleri behind the queen, wishing she could be somewhere, anywhere else. Her stomach hurt and she felt light-headed, but the queen had insisted that she come to the feast along with Tegan and Maeve and Garwen. Eleri was clearly worried about her sister, and hung on to Rhianna tightly. Rhianna simply stared ahead, trying not to think about the horrors she had seen earlier, and failing.

After a time, the queen rose to her feet and the crowd fell silent. 'We have won a great victory today!' she said, and the crowd roared. The queen raised her hands and they grew quiet again. 'But we must not forget we owe it all to the goddess.

I dedicate the dead of the battle to her, and I will also offer her more. Viducos, bring forward half the prisoners... Who among you wants to be their executioners?'

The crowd roared as Viducos did the queen's bidding. The prisoners were dragged in front of her and a dozen warriors emerged from the crowd with swords drawn. Rhianna noticed one of them was Segovax before she turned away, bile rising in her throat and filling her mouth with a foul taste. She fixed her eyes on Garwen, pleading with her wordlessly for help. Garwen met her gaze and instantly understood.

'My lady, I think Rhianna is feeling unwell again,' she said. 'Perhaps it would be better if I took her and Eleri back to their tent so they can both rest...'

'Fine, do as you wish,' said the queen, clearly cross. 'But Rhianna, you will need a stronger stomach if you are to stay in my service, and that of the goddess.'

Rhianna said nothing, and Garwen helped her and Eleri to their feet. Eleri looked towards

Maeve, clearly hoping for a goodnight hug and kiss from the queen's daughter. But Maeve and Tegan were standing beside their mother, and Maeve took no notice of Eleri. Instead, she glared at the Romans on their knees, then she and Tegan suddenly started screaming wildly, their faces distorted with hatred.

'Kill them! Kill them for the goddess! Kill them! *Kill them!*'

Eleri recoiled and began to cry. Rhianna pulled her closer, and Garwen hurried them away through the camp. The crowd was roaring once more, and chanting now as well. Rhianna felt the noise like a powerful wave pushing her from behind.

They came to their tent and Rhianna took Eleri inside, yet it was a while before she got her settled. Eleri was still upset, and they could still hear the crowd, but she fell asleep at last. Rhianna kissed her gently and stepped out of the tent again.

'Is she all right?' said Garwen, who was waiting for her. The glow of the big fire at the feast lit up the night sky, but it was dark in this part of the camp.

'I think she will be,' said Rhianna, frowning. 'So long as I keep her away from Maeve that is. How could Maeve be like that? She's not the same person she was.'

'You might be a different person if you had suffered as Maeve and her sister have done,' said Garwen. 'After such terrible pain it is easy to hate the people who hurt you. Imagine how you would feel if the Romans had whipped you, or Eleri.'

Rhianna could see the truth behind Garwen's words. 'But why has it made them so cruel?' she said. 'It almost seems as if Maeve and Tegan want to kill *every* Roman, not just the ones who beat them. And I don't really understand why the queen thinks the goddess wants so many sacrifices, so much blood.'

'I'm not sure I understand it either…' said Garwen, lowering her head. Then she looked up and squared her shoulders. 'But she is still my queen, and I have to believe she knows the goddess better than I do. Remember, the Romans are cruel too.'

Their eyes locked for a moment and it was Rhianna's turn to shrug. 'You are right, Garwen,' she said. 'But it was hard for me to see what happened today. I just don't think I can be as strong as the queen wants. And I fear for Eleri in all of this.'

'I can offer you no help with that, Rhianna.' The noise of the crowd grew louder and Garwen glanced towards the distant fire. 'We all walk with fear as a companion now. But I know you will do everything in your power to protect your sister.'

They talked a while longer, then Garwen said goodnight and returned to the queen. Rhianna ducked back into the tent and lay beside Eleri. She prayed to the goddess, the one her mother had always spoken of, asking her to make things better...

But there was much worse to come.

CHAPTER EIGHT
Blood and Fire

T wo days later they reached a low ridge from where they could see Camulodunum. Rhianna was in the queen's wagon as usual, Eleri sitting beside her. The Roman city was much larger than Rhianna had expected, perhaps twice as big as the Royal Place of the Iceni. It was surrounded with a similar ditch and mound of earth, but had no stockade or walls for protection, and the houses were strangely different too. Most appeared to be made of square stones, and had roofs of reddish-brown tiles.

A giant building stood in the heart of the settlement, like a great white bull rising above a flock of sheep – Rhianna realised it must be the Temple of Claudius. There were steps leading up to an entrance behind a row of white columns that reflected the morning sun, almost dazzling her. Gold gleamed in the fantastic carvings of gods that filled the space above the columns and below the roof. Rhianna thought the Romans must possess godlike skills themselves to have created such a building.

The queen was standing a little way off with Viducos, Andorix and Cumenal. They were talking and Cumenal was waving his arms around, pointing at the city that once belonged to his tribe. Rhianna turned to look behind her at the huge crowd waiting with the chariots and the rest of the wagons. Boudica had ordered everyone to call it the war-host from now on, to show that the peoples of all three tribes were fighting together. There was much chatter and laughter – Rhianna could feel the excitement rising in them.

She jumped off the wagon and went over to ask Garwen what was going on. Garwen was in her chariot, staring at the city with a thoughtful expression, the other body servants drawn up around her in their chariots. The horses were excited too – they were stamping and snorting and tossing their heads, their manes flying.

'Cumenal's spies in the city have sent a message,' said Garwen. 'Decianus dispatched some soldiers here from Londinium when he heard we were coming. But there are only two hundred at most, so they cannot stop us taking the city.'

'What will happen then?' said Rhianna, even though she could guess.

'There will be blood and fire,' said Garwen with a shrug. She turned to Rhianna and looked into her eyes. 'Most of the women and children will wait here while the warriors attack. I think you and your sister should stay here as well.'

At that moment the queen called to Garwen, and she drove her chariot over to her. Rhianna ran back to the queen's wagon, her stomach suddenly twisting with fear again. Viducos started to yell orders, and the warriors moved forward, heading towards the city, walking at first, but soon breaking into a run. Now Rhianna could make out the Roman soldiers, small groups of men waiting behind flimsy barricades of overturned wagons and carts. Eleri reached for her hand and held it tight.

Rhianna had already realised this would not be a battle for the chariots. The foot warriors swept through them and beyond like a great living wave, screaming their hatred for the Romans. They crashed into the barricades, and then there was a chaos of noise and struggle, blades clashing and people yelling. Garwen had been right, of course – the defenders were quickly wiped out. Before long Rhianna saw lines of warriors hurrying up the narrow streets that led to the Temple of Claudius.

Word came back to those watching from the ridge that most of the city's people had barricaded themselves inside the temple. Rhianna heard somebody saying the Romans were probably counting on holding out behind the temple's thick doors and walls long enough for Paulinus to arrive with his army. There was little chance of that, though. It seemed that Paulinus and his legions were still far away in Mona.

Rhianna tried to stay on the ridge so that neither she nor her sister would see any horrors. But the queen sent a message summoning her, so she reluctantly set off with Eleri. Luckily, Garwen met them as they walked towards the city and whisked Eleri off for a ride in her chariot, much to Rhianna's relief.

The queen was sitting in a chair taken from one of the houses. Tegan and Maeve were standing on either side of her, and the three of them were guarded by half a dozen body servants. They were watching some warriors hacking at the temple's great oak doors with axes. Rhianna felt nervous as she approached the queen. Boudica had been angry with her at the feast after the first battle, and had barely spoken to her since.

But now the queen smiled at her. 'Ah, Rhianna, I am glad you could join us,' she said. 'I feel I should apologise again – I might have been too hard on you. I still believe the goddess brought you to me for a good reason, that somehow our fates are linked... So I will give you another chance to serve me, and the goddess.'

'Thank you,' said Rhianna. She was surprised, but relieved for a second time that morning. 'I will do my best to serve you, my lady, and the goddess too, of course.'

'I know you will,' said the queen, her eyes locking on to Rhianna's for an instant, before she returned her attention to the temple. 'You will also soon realise how lucky you are to be with me, Rhianna. You are going to see such amazing things.'

But what Rhianna saw next was the stuff of nightmares.

* * *

It took quite a while to work out how to break into the temple. In the end Viducos realised the weak point was the roof, and ordered ladders to be made so the warriors could climb up. They ripped off the tiles and dropped flaming torches through the holes on to the people below, or shot arrows at them. Before long the doors flew open and hundreds of Romans ran out – straight into a crowd of warriors.

The queen was still sitting in the chair, flanked by Tegan and Maeve, the three of them looking on as the warriors laughed at the Romans or screamed in their faces. Rhianna was standing behind the queen and saw how frightened the Romans looked, the mothers clinging to their children, trying to protect them from the baying mob. Blades flashed, and now the Romans were crying and begging for mercy.

'Viducos, a word with you!' the queen called out. Viducos turned at the sound of her voice, then walked slowly over to her, a look of irritation on his face.

'I can guess what you're going to say, Boudica,' he said. 'You don't want them all killed. I'll talk to Cumenal, but the Trinovantes have a lot of old scores to settle, so it might be tricky. They have scented Roman blood and they want more.'

'Just do your best, Viducos,' said the queen. 'I need them for…'

'I know, for the goddess,' said Viducos, rolling his eyes. 'I only hope that all your sacrifices mean she will help us when Paulinus turns up, as he most certainly will.'

'Why, Viducos, it almost sounds as if you fear him.' The queen was now looking at Viducos with a raised eyebrow. 'Surely we have proved that the Romans are no match for us. We have slaughtered their soldiers on the field and easily taken this place.'

'Of course I fear Paulinus,' said Viducos. 'It is one thing to ambush less than a third of a legion, or to take a city that has hardly any defenders. Paulinus will have had time to prepare now, and I know what it is like to fight a proper Roman army.'

The queen smiled, but Rhianna saw that her eyes were cold and hard. 'You men never learn, do you?' said the queen. 'You lost to the Romans before because you stopped worshipping the goddess. Believe me, after the sacrifices I am going to offer her she will *ensure* we destroy them utterly. The day of reckoning is at hand.'

Viducos sighed. 'No, Boudica, we lost to the Romans because they are better at war than us. We've had it easy so far, but it's not going to stay that way…'

They argued a while longer, but eventually Viducos did as he was told and went to speak with Cumenal. Rhianna saw Cumenal react angrily, yet he gave in, allowing Viducos to choose fifty Romans as future sacrifices and lead them away. There were terrible scenes as families were brutally divided – husbands and wives, parents and children screaming out for each other in fear and panic…

The horror went on into the night, and the queen insisted that Rhianna stay with her. Houses were set on fire, so the air was full of smoke and cinders. Warriors drank wine from the big jars they found and smashed open, and danced to the drums of the Druids. Sometimes Romans were flushed out of hiding, and Rhianna saw terrible things done to them. Yet she dared not flinch or look away in front of the queen – and at that moment Rhianna realised she didn't much like Boudica any more.

She felt a surge of guilt at the thought. Boudica was her queen, so she should be loyal to her, shouldn't she? Besides, the queen had saved her and Eleri, taking them in when they had nowhere else to go. That had seemed kind and loving... but Boudica had turned out to be cold-hearted. Of course the Romans had been cruel to her and her daughters, so Rhianna understood why she wanted revenge. But all of this killing in the name of the goddess was wrong – especially as Boudica clearly enjoyed it.

Then Rhianna felt another wave of guilt, about Eleri this time. After Magunna had thrown them out, accepting the queen's offer to take them in had seemed the best plan, a perfect way of keeping Eleri safe. Now Rhianna was starting to realise it might be the worst thing she could have done to her sister. There was deadly danger all around them, and it was getting worse with every day that went past.

What if the queen turned against her permanently? What would happen to her and Eleri then? What if Paulinus defeated the war-host?

Viducos obviously believed it was possible, perhaps even likely, and Rhianna had a nasty feeling that the Romans would not forgive the tribes for what they had done here at Camulodunum. So there would be more killing to come.

As she stood behind the seated queen, Rhianna felt her eyes begin to fill with tears. She and Eleri were trapped in this dreadful nightmare – and it was all her fault. Why had she not taken Garwen's advice and asked the queen to send Eleri to the safe place in the marshes? Then her sister at least would be far from this madness – the slaughter and destruction, the crackling flames, the choking black smoke…

'Why are you crying, Rhianna?' Boudica said, breaking into her thoughts. The queen had turned round and was staring at her with narrowed eyes. Tegan and Maeve were staring at her too, their faces pale and blank, almost like those of the dead.

Rhianna said nothing for a moment, terrified the queen could somehow look into her mind and see what she was thinking. Her heart pounded, and it felt as if their lives might depend on what she said next. Suddenly she thought of asking the goddess for help – not the queen's goddess, her mother's kind and loving goddess instead.

She prayed silently to her, and a simple reply came straight back.

'*You must be careful not to give yourself away*,' said the goddess in her mind, although the voice was her mother's. '*Think of a reason for your tears…*'

Rhianna did just that, and wiped her face with the sleeve of her gown. 'I am not crying, my lady,' she said. 'My eyes are watering because of the smoke.'

'Is that so?' The queen's voice was soft, but she stared at Rhianna for just a little longer. 'Well then, we should leave before your eyes grow worse,' she said. 'Come, girls. It has been an exciting day, and now it is time for us to rest.'

The queen rose from her chair and strode off between the burning houses with her daughters, three dark figures outlined by the light of the flames, the guard of body servants around them.

Rhianna followed closely behind, and soon they emerged from the city. Back on the ridge, Rhianna saw that the queen's tent had been put up. Garwen was there too, but without Eleri, and Rhianna felt a stab of worry.

Garwen was quick to reassure her, however. 'Eleri is asleep in your tent, Rhianna,' she said quietly. 'And she has seen nothing today that will disturb her dreams.'

'Thank you,' said Rhianna, and hurried away. Garwen had put up their tent in its usual place, just behind the queen's, and Rhianna ducked inside the entrance. As Garwen had said, Eleri was fast asleep, and Rhianna lay down beside her. Rhianna wished they were far away from this place, and the war-host, and the queen...

Suddenly Rhianna realised that was the answer.

She and Eleri had to escape.

CHAPTER NINE
Burning and Looting

The queen gave the order for the war-host to leave Camulodunum the next day. It took time for everyone to assemble, so it was late in the morning before they set off. Rhianna was in the queen's wagon with Eleri, and looked back at the city as they rode away. A great pall of smoke hung over it, the darkness rising to fill the blue sky. Memories of what she had seen filled Rhianna's mind, and she quickly turned her head.

Yet she felt happier than she had done for a long while. Things were bad, of course, but at least she had a plan, or the beginnings of one at any rate. They were going to escape from Boudica and the war-host as soon as possible. It was only a question of working out how, and that shouldn't be too hard. In the meantime she would just have to make sure the queen didn't suspect what she had in mind.

Boudica was leading the war-host, riding with Garwen in her chariot. They were heading south-west, along a road the Romans had built after they had beaten the Trinovantes and captured Camulodunum. It was wide and perfectly straight, its surface of stones stretching ahead as far as Rhianna could see. Making roads was obviously something else the Romans did very well, she thought.

'Are we going home now, Rhianna?' said Eleri. 'I'm fed up with riding in this horrible old wagon. And I don't like sleeping in that tent, it's too small…'

Rhianna turned to her sister. Eleri looked pale and tired, and Rhianna hoped she wasn't sickening for something. Eleri certainly wasn't excited any more, and was clearly bored most of the time, except when she was frightened. For a moment Rhianna felt an urge to tell her what she was planning, if only to cheer her up. But that would be a mistake. What if Eleri let it slip in front of the queen?

'I'm sorry,' Rhianna said, hugging her. 'We're not going home just yet.'

Rhianna said no more. She didn't have the heart to tell Eleri she was no longer sure where their home might be. If they did get away, Rhianna knew Boudica would never forgive them, so they couldn't return to the Royal Place. In fact, they might not be able to go anywhere in the lands of the Iceni, which meant they would have to find a home with another tribe – and that would be hard.

Rhianna couldn't bring herself to tell Eleri they were heading for Londinium either. She had heard Viducos and Boudica arguing about it earlier.

'Listen, Boudica, I like burning Roman cities as much as anyone,' said Viducos. 'But we would be much better off finding Paulinus before he finishes his preparations.'

'How many times do I have to tell you, Viducos?' said the queen. 'Paulinus is doomed whatever he does. We will scour the Romans from all Britannia!'

They had even talked of moving on to a third city, Verulamium – Andorix was particularly keen for the war-host to go there. It had once been the main stronghold of the Catuvellauni, but the Romans had cast them out and made the place their own. It seemed therefore that Boudica had a plan as well, Rhianna thought, although the queen's would definitely involve rather more blood and fire than hers.

Rhianna spent the rest of the day doing her best to lift Eleri's mood. She talked and sang and played lots of games with her. Every so often Rhianna looked around, observing the war-host, searching for a way to escape. And gradually her own mood began to sink as she saw it might not be quite so easy as she had imagined…

The war-host was enormous, and it was growing all the time. Many more of the Trinovantes had joined it at Camulodunum, and others flocked to them from each village they passed. Slipping away unnoticed through such a vast horde would be easy for most people, Rhianna thought. But everyone knew she was a favourite of the queen, and that Eleri was her little sister. They would be recognised wherever they went – and somebody was sure to tell the queen if they were seen leaving.

Rhianna didn't like to think how the queen would punish them if that happened, but it would be bad. They would only get one chance to escape, so they couldn't fail.

Rhianna sighed as the wagon creaked along. Why did everything have to be so difficult? Then she found herself looking at the Roman captives, and she realised they were much worse off than her and Eleri. At least a hundred Roman men, women and children trudged along in the middle of the war-host, their faces full of fear. Viducos spoke some Latin, and Boudica had got him to tell them they were all going to be sacrificed to the goddess. Rhianna thought that had seemed particularly cruel.

Two captives caught her eye, a young woman and a girl of Eleri's age. They were both dark-haired and slim, and both wore white gowns that must once have been fine but were now dirty and torn. Rhianna guessed they were mother and daughter, and her heart almost broke at the thought of how terrified the mother must be for her child. The woman stared at Rhianna across the crowd, their eyes locking together for an instant. Rhianna looked away. She had enough worries of her own…

According to Garwen, it should have taken three, perhaps four days for the war-host to reach Londinium. But six days later they still hadn't got there, although nobody seemed to care that much. They had come across several Roman farms and burned them, killing the farmers and their families if they hadn't fled, taking their cattle and sheep to add to the war-host's food stocks. Rhianna tried to make sure Eleri didn't see the worst things, but that was getting harder all the time.

For a while Rhianna convinced herself that the best way to escape would be after the war-host made camp each day. Yet she soon realised that wouldn't work either – the evening feasts went on till dawn, with drumming and drinking and dancing, and nobody seemed to sleep. The Roman captives were divided into small groups and kept tied up in different parts of the camp, so it would be hard for them to escape too, Rhianna thought. The only good thing was that there were no more sacrifices.

'I am saving the captives for the right moment,' Rhianna heard the queen telling Viducos one night. Warriors were dancing around a huge fire, sparks rising from it into the black sky. The drums pounded and the war-host seemed wilder than ever.

'And when will that be?' said Viducos, staring at Boudica, his arms crossed.

'When we have enough Romans to show the goddess just how much we worship her,' said the queen, the red firelight reflected in her eyes. 'Imagine how pleased she will be if we sacrifice hundreds of Romans to her all at the same time! I will give the order when we finally face Paulinus and his soldiers – it will terrify them.'

'You're wrong,' said Viducos, shaking his head. 'It will just make them angry – and also realise they have to defeat us or risk suffering the same fate. We have to be cleverer than that, Boudica, or we might as well give in to Paulinus now…'

Rhianna thought briefly of all the Roman captives being slaughtered at once, and pushed the image out of her mind. It was a warm night, but she still shivered.

* * *

The war-host reached Londinium two days later. It was smaller than Camulodunum, a compact cluster of buildings on a couple of low hills that looked down on to the broad River Tamesis. A rough stockade surrounded the city, but the gates were wide open and the scouts reported there were no soldiers to defend the place. So the war-host swept in, and the burning and looting and killing began all over again.

Boudica took over the house of Decianus, the Roman who had come to the Royal Place and ordered the whipping of the queen and her daughters. It was a large building on one side of the city's marketplace, or Forum as the Romans called it. But the procurator himself was long gone. Some of his slaves were still in the house, and they told the queen Decianus had fled, leaving on the same day the news came that she had taken Camulodunum. He had loaded a ship with gold he had stolen for himself and fled to Gaul.

'You see, Rhianna?' said the queen. 'He is a coward, like all Romans.'

Rhianna said nothing, but she wasn't sure Boudica was right about all Romans being cowards. According to the slaves, Paulinus had been in Londinium a few days ago. He had destroyed the Druids on Mona, and had ordered his army to march south as quickly as possible.

But he himself had ridden ahead with a small cavalry escort – no more than ten men – to Londinium before the war-host arrived.

'It was a brave thing to do,' Garwen said. She and Rhianna were in the house of Decianus, looking out of a big window at the city. Night had fallen, flames leaped from a few of the houses nearby and Rhianna could hear screams of fear and pain. 'He might have run into our scouts at any time,' Garwen went on. 'But he knew he had to see how things really are. I think this Paulinus is a very good war leader.'

'He didn't stay though, did he?' said Rhianna. 'He left the day he arrived.'

'That was probably his plan,' said Garwen, shrugging. 'He came to find out what he could, and to tell the people to leave. More should have listened to him…'

Rhianna agreed with her. Many Romans had stayed in Londinium and over the next three days most of them died. On the fourth morning Boudica led the war-host out of the city, a pall of black smoke filling the sky. They headed north on the Roman road to Verulamium, and five days later that city was burning too.

By the time the war-host left Verulamium and made camp beyond it, at one end of a valley, Rhianna was almost in despair. She was beginning to think there was no way out for her and Eleri, that this nightmare would go on forever. Eleri had also now seen terrible things that she didn't understand and Rhianna couldn't explain. That night Rhianna barely slept, and at dawn she decided to ask Garwen for help.

Eleri too had been restless, but she was fast asleep at last. Rhianna left the tent carefully so as not to wake her, and went to find Garwen. The camp was quiet, with only a few people stirring, a baby crying somewhere. Garwen's tent stood next to the queen's, and Rhianna was about to go inside when she heard the sound of pounding feet. She looked round and saw a warrior running towards the queen's tent.

'My lady!' he called out, coming to a halt but not daring to go in. He was young, his long dark hair tied back in a ponytail, his eyes wide with excitement. 'The Romans... the Romans have just appeared at the other end of the valley!'

'What are you talking about?' said Garwen. She stepped out of her tent, already buckling on her sword-belt as she spoke. 'Is it Paulinus and his army?'

'Viducos thinks it is,' said the warrior. 'It looks like at least two legions.'

The queen came out of her tent, followed by Tegan and Maeve. 'Why did our scouts not bring us a warning?' said Boudica. 'Isn't that what they're for?'

'Paulinus probably told his scouts to hunt ours down and kill them,' said Garwen. 'It's the kind of thing a good commander does if he wants to surprise his enemy.'

The queen gave her a hard look – but then she smiled. 'It doesn't matter how good a commander Paulinus is, he will be no match for the goddess,' she said. 'Boy, take me to Viducos. I must speak with him and see this Roman army for myself. I want you at my side, Garwen. We will need to start organising the war-host...'

The warrior nodded and headed in the direction from which he had come, with Boudica sweeping after him with her daughters. Rhianna watched her go, this proud Iceni queen in her rich green cloak, her red hair glowing in the early morning light, and for a moment the old love she had felt for her briefly returned. But then it faded again and she was filled with fear at the thought of what was about to happen.

'Listen to me, Rhianna,' said Garwen. She gripped Rhianna's arm and turned her round so they were facing each other. 'Where is Eleri? You must get away.'

'She is in our tent,' said Rhianna. 'I was coming to ask for your help. I've wanted to take Eleri away for several days now, but I didn't think we could escape. I was sure someone would tell the queen if we tried and that she wouldn't let us leave.'

'Everyone will be too busy now to worry about you,' said Rhianna. 'Head for the woods on the side of the valley. Find somewhere to hide until dark, then get as far from here as you can before the sun rises. Good fortune to you, Rhianna.'

Garwen gave her a brief hug, then turned and ran off after the queen. Rhianna wondered if she would ever see Garwen again, but there was no time to brood about it. The whole camp was coming to life, people calling out, horses whinnying…

Rhianna ran back to her tent to wake Eleri.

CHAPTER TEN

Fifty Silent Warriors

'But why do we have to leave, Rhianna?' said Eleri. 'I don't understand.'

It had taken Rhianna a while to rouse her. Now Eleri stood looking confused and full of sleep. Rhianna was bustling round the tent, finding their cloaks and stuffing bread and cheese and their few possessions in a bag. She didn't have time for lengthy explanations – best to keep it simple. 'The Romans are coming and bad things will happen,' she said. 'So we really need to get away from here – all right?'

Eleri nodded, properly awake at last, her eyes wide with fear. They slipped out of the tent and headed through the camp towards the woods. Garwen had spoken the truth, of course – nobody took any notice of them. Groups of warriors hurried past, moving deeper into the valley where the fighting would take place. Most of the women were going in the opposite direction, herding their children back to the wagons that had been drawn up in a semi-circle across the entrance to the valley.

The noise had increased – people were yelling, chariot drivers whistling to their horses, mothers calling for lost children. A light breeze was bringing thick clouds from the west and the sky was steadily darkening. Suddenly Rhianna heard a loud blaring in the distance, like a herd of bulls bellowing, and a chill ran down her spine.

'That'll be the Roman war-horns,' she heard a grizzled old warrior saying to a younger man. 'They must be getting into their line of battle already…'

Rhianna wasn't sure what that meant, but it didn't sound good, so she pulled Eleri along more quickly. They passed through a cluster of small tents and shelters made from branches and came to a patch of open ground. A small group of Roman captives was sitting there, perhaps a dozen people, their hands tied behind them with rawhide strips. As Rhianna and Eleri went by, a young woman looked up. There was a little girl at her side and Rhianna realised they were the two she had noticed before.

'Help us, I beg you!' said the woman, her voice full of panic and terror. She spoke Rhianna's tongue with a strong accent, but didn't mangle the words like Decianus. 'Please, untie us! I must save my daughter – she doesn't deserve to die…'

Rhianna stopped, her attention caught, and stared at her. For the space of a few heartbeats everything seemed to slow down, the noise around them fading – and at that moment Rhianna understood there was no difference between her and this Roman woman. They were both trying to save somebody they loved in a world full of madness and death. Yet Rhianna knew she should hurry on, make sure Eleri was safe. The woods were so close, the first trees only a hundred paces up the slope…

'Please…' the woman said quietly, her eyes glistening with tears.

Rhianna heard a voice in her mind. She couldn't tell if it was the goddess or her mother, but it didn't matter who was speaking, the words were quite clear. *Don't let them be killed, Rhianna. You won't be able to live with yourself if you do.*

She reached into her bag and pulled out her mother's little knife. The woman recoiled, then immediately scrambled to put her body between Rhianna and her daughter.

'Don't worry, I won't hurt you,' Rhianna said, smiling to reassure her. 'Turn round and I'll cut you free.' The woman did as she was told, and Rhianna quickly sliced through the tight rawhide strips on her wrists and those binding the girl.

'Thank you,' said the woman. She stood up and helped her daughter to her feet. 'You have done a good thing today. I pray that the gods will keep you safe.'

Then she took her daughter's hand and they ran towards the woods. Rhianna watched them go… and then the noise of the war-host came flooding back, and soon the rest of the captives were calling out, begging her to release them too. They shuffled towards her, clambering over each other, pushing each other aside in fear and desperation, and she tried to do what they asked. But it was impossible.

'Hey, what are you doing?' somebody yelled. 'Get away from them!'

Rhianna looked round and her heart nearly leaped out of her mouth – a dozen warriors armed with spears were dashing towards her. 'Run, Eleri!' she yelled, but Eleri shook her head and stayed where she was. By the time Rhianna got to her it was too late – the warriors were all around them. Rhianna tried to fight them off, but they grabbed her, making her drop the knife, and soon they were both held fast.

'Only a couple made it to the woods,' said one of the warriors. 'Shall we go after them? I'll bet the queen knows exactly how many she's supposed to have.'

'No, there won't be time before the battle starts,' said the man who had yelled at Rhianna to get away from the captives. She recognised his voice now and felt true despair. Being caught was bad enough, but being caught by *him* made it much worse. 'Besides, we needn't worry about losing a few,' he went on. 'I'm sure the queen will be happy to see this one and her sister – won't she, Rhianna?'

It was Segovax, and he was very pleased with himself indeed.

* * *

The warriors bound Rhianna and Eleri, the rawhide tight on their wrists. Eleri was tearful, and Rhianna tried to comfort her, but she couldn't say much before they were dragged off with the rest of the captives. 'Magunna won't want to miss this,' said Segovax with a cheerful grin, and sent one of the warriors to fetch her. Then he led the captives back through the camp. Eventually they came to the last of the tents, but Segovax kept right on going, leading them further out into the open valley.

It was like a shallow grassy bowl, the slope on one side rising to a rocky ridge, and on the other to the woods, the trees blending into a dark mass. Below her, Rhianna could see another mass filling this end of the valley, one made of thousands of men and women – the war-host. There was movement in it, ripples passing through as warriors pressed forward. The noise was much louder here – everyone seemed to be yelling and screaming and banging swords and spear shafts on their shields.

Most of the chariots were drawn up in a line along the front of the war-host, with a smaller group standing beyond them. These few were driven by the queen's body servants, and had been arranged in the shape of an arrowhead – a back row of four, then three, then two, and finally one to be the sharp point aimed at the enemy. It was hard to make out much detail at such a distance, yet Rhianna knew the tall, straight-backed driver of that leading chariot could only be Garwen.

'Come on, girl, don't just stand there gawping,' said Segovax, shoving Rhianna hard between the shoulder blades. 'Or would you like me to kill you here?'

Eleri gasped, but Rhianna turned and glared at him. 'You wouldn't dare,' she said. 'I am the queen's favourite and she won't believe a single word you say.'

Segovax smirked. 'There might have been a time when the queen liked you, but you're not her favourite any more,' he said. 'Magunna and I have seen how she has grown tired of you. Now move, or prepare to die. I'll be happy either way.'

Rhianna knew she had no choice but to obey. So she walked on, thinking hard all the time, trying to come up with a new plan to get them out of this mess. Perhaps she should fall on her knees before the queen, admit what she had done and beg her forgiveness. If that worked, then she and Eleri might be able to make a run for it later, when the queen and everyone else would probably be distracted by the battle…

The queen was behind the war-host, standing on a grassy mound so she could see over their heads and down the valley, with Tegan and Maeve on either side of her. Viducos was at the base of the mound with Andorix and Cumenal, all three stripped to the waist like the rest of the warriors, their tattoos dark against pale skin. Segovax halted the captives in front of them, but pulled Rhianna up the mound to the queen.

'My lady, I caught this girl helping some of the Romans to escape,' he said. 'I think she and her sister were planning to run away from the war-host as well.'

'Is this true, Rhianna?' said the queen. She was outlined against the iron-grey sky, her hair blown backwards in the breeze like flames streaming out behind her. She was wearing her finest gown and cloak, and her golden torc gleamed at her throat.

'It is, my lady,' said Rhianna, looking into her eyes. 'But I can explain…'

'There is no need,' the queen said, her face a mask of fury. 'I thought the goddess had brought us together for a reason, but clearly I was wrong.

You have betrayed me, but you have betrayed the goddess too – and I can never forgive you for that.'

Something snapped inside Rhianna then, and she felt angry too. She knew she shouldn't give in to it, but she just couldn't stop herself – she had to speak her mind.

'I'm not the one who has betrayed the goddess, it's you!' she said. 'My mother taught me that the goddess is kind and loving – she doesn't want all these sacrifices, all this blood. You're only doing it because you're cruel and you like it!'

'Ah, now I understand your sulks and silences,' said the queen. 'Your mother didn't really know the goddess then. The truth she teaches us is that life is a constant struggle. Only those who are more cruel than their enemies will survive.'

'You're wrong,' said Rhianna, shaking her head. 'I know that in my heart.'

'It is your soft heart that will be your downfall, Rhianna,' the queen said quietly. Then she turned to Segovax. 'How many captives did she help to escape?'

'Only two, my lady,' said Segovax. 'They got into the woods before…'

The queen silenced him with a wave of her hand. 'I see the will of the goddess in this,' she said, smiling. 'She works in mysterious ways. You let two of my captives go, Rhianna, so you and your sister will replace them. Take them to join the others.'

'No… you can't do that to us!' Rhianna screamed, but the queen and Tegan and Maeve stared at her with faces of stone. Segovax grabbed Rhianna and dragged her back down the mound to the warriors holding Eleri and the other captives.

Just then Magunna arrived, panting after having run from the wagons. She came right up to Rhianna and slapped her face. Rhianna staggered backwards, but Segovax stopped her falling. 'I've wanted to do that for so long,' Magunna said, reaching round to pull the rings from Rhianna's fingers. 'What did the queen say?' Magunna asked Segovax. 'I hope she's going to punish the two of them properly.'

'Oh yes,' said Segovax, grinning. 'They're to be sacrificed with the Romans.'

'I'm glad to hear it,' said Magunna, leaning forward, her nose almost touching Rhianna's. 'You should have been drowned at birth, like unwanted puppies.'

Rhianna opened her mouth to reply, hatred for Magunna boiling inside her. But Segovax didn't give her the chance. 'This way,' he said, plunging into the war-host, dragging Rhianna with him, her cheek stinging, his men bringing the other captives in their wake. Rhianna looked round, trying to keep Eleri in sight. But there were too many people, the smell of their sweat filling Rhianna's nostrils. Some of them jostled her and screamed curses and insults in her face. She thought she was going to be sick, but eventually they left the crowd behind.

They passed through the chariots, emerging to the left of the arrowhead group. Rhianna glimpsed Garwen, but Garwen was looking up the valley and didn't see her. Segovax kept going, and Rhianna saw where he was heading. The Roman captives were even further out, beyond the chariots, two hundred men, women and children, all on their knees. Fifty silent warriors with drawn swords stood behind them.

Segovax came to a halt at last. Rhianna looked round once more, searching for her sister, and saw her being dragged out of the war-host, a warrior bringing her over to Segovax. Rhianna shook Segovax off and pressed herself as close as she could to Eleri, kissing the warm top of her head, breathing in her familiar scent, both of them sobbing. But Rhianna's mind was still working hard, still desperately trying to think of a way out of all this. She refused to believe they had reached their end…

'What a glorious moment!' said Segovax. He rammed his spear blade-down into the ground and drew his sword. 'The gods will give us a great victory today…'

Suddenly Rhianna realised he was distracted – and that gave her a chance. So she hooked a foot round his ankles and knocked him backwards with her shoulder, just as Garwen had taught her. Segovax fell heavily, crashing to the ground with a thump.

'Quick, Eleri, follow me!' Rhianna yelled, and they set off running.

Only Garwen could save them now.

CHAPTER ELEVEN

Nothing But Death

R hianna quickly discovered it was almost impossible to run properly with your hands tied behind your back. Eleri was finding it hard as well, and Rhianna had to keep stopping to try and hurry her along. Yet Garwen in her chariot seemed just as far away as ever. Soon Rhianna realised Segovax had recovered and was slowly getting to his feet. His men had seen what had happened, and several had stepped forward to help him. Some were pointing at her and Eleri, drawing attention to them.

'Garwen!' Rhianna yelled, but there was too much noise coming from the war-host for Garwen to hear her. Suddenly another sound was added to the clamour, the same bull-like blaring Rhianna had heard earlier. But this time it was so loud she felt it like a blow. She came to a halt and turned to look for the source – and that's when she saw the Romans. Their shields formed a solid wall right across the opposite end of the valley, each one bearing the image of two crossed lightning flashes.

Only a few hundred paces of open ground separated the war-host and the Romans, yet there was all the difference in the world between them. The war-host seethed with noise and movement, but the Romans were silent and watchful. The Roman end of the valley sloped upwards too, so Rhianna could see a dozen standard-bearers behind the front line, bearskins over their heads and shoulders, the eagles standing proud. Beside each one were men carrying war-horns, great curved instruments of shining bronze.

Beyond them was a small group of men on horses, one man more noticeable than the rest.

His golden breastplate shone even in the dull light, and his helmet had a red crest bigger than anybody else's. Rhianna guessed she was looking at Paulinus himself, but she had no time to study him. He raised his hand, a group of archers stepped up from behind him – and shot their arrows into the air. The deadly missiles rose with a terrifying buzzing noise… then dropped on to the war-host.

Warriors fell, screaming in agony, and Rhianna felt doom approaching like a great dark wave. Segovax was up and running, making for her and Eleri, his sword drawn and his face grim. Rhianna nudged Eleri ahead and yelled at Garwen once more, shouting her name so loudly that her throat hurt. And this time Garwen heard, or perhaps it was just that she had turned to watch the flight of the arrows and caught sight of Rhianna and Eleri. She came racing in her chariot towards them.

'What are you doing here?' she said, reining in the horses, the chariot now between Rhianna and Eleri and the war-host. 'You were supposed to have got away!'

'I tried, but Segovax caught us and took us to the queen,' said Rhianna. 'I set two captives free, so she told Segovax to sacrifice Eleri and me in their place…'

'She speaks the truth – for once,' said Segovax, appearing at that moment. 'I was going to kill you quickly. After your little trick, however, I think I'll make it slow.'

He advanced on Rhianna and Eleri, his sword raised, but Garwen jumped from her chariot and stood between him and them, her hand on the hilt of her own sword.

'Don't come any closer,' she said. 'Not unless you want to die, that is.'

'Ah, now I understand,' said Segovax, grinning. 'You've been teaching the little vixen some of your tricks. Well, you won't catch me like that a third time…'

Suddenly he stepped forward, swinging his sword at Garwen's head, the blade whistling through the air. Garwen swayed backwards, the tip of the blade only just missing her cheek, and whipped out her sword to strike back at him. Segovax raised his, the blades ringing as they clashed, and they exchanged more blows, Garwen light on her feet, almost like a dancer, Rhianna thought. Segovax was strong and powerful, those muscles in his arms rippling, but he had none of Garwen's skill or grace.

Soon he was panting and grunting, hardly able to believe he was losing against a woman – and then it was over. Garwen dodged a wild stroke, then rammed her blade right through him. She pulled it out and he fell to the ground, a threat no more.

Rhianna realised she had been holding her breath all through the fight, and now she let it go. Garwen sheathed her sword and came over, drawing her dagger to cut the rawhide strips binding Rhianna and Eleri. 'Quickly, into the chariot,' she said.

They did as they were told, Rhianna helping Eleri up, Garwen joining them. She pulled the reins, tugging the horses round so the chariot faced the wooded side of the valley, and soon it was racing between the Romans and the war-host.

Rhianna held on tight to Eleri, expecting to be chased. But the nearest warriors just seemed confused, and she realised that only the Romans had seen the fight. Then the Roman archers fired more arrows, and everybody stopped looking at Garwen's chariot.

She stopped at the bottom of the slope and turned to Rhianna. 'Out you get,' she said. 'Make for the woods, and this time keep running till you're far away.'

Rhianna jumped off the chariot and helped Eleri down. 'Come with us, Garwen,' Rhianna said, looking up at her. 'There is nothing here for you, nothing but...'

She couldn't finish what she wanted to say. It was almost as if by speaking the word she might actually make it happen, and that thought was too painful.

'Nothing but death?' said Garwen, smiling at her. 'I have lived with the idea I might die in the queen's service since the day I made my vow to her. I will not break it now – but I will die more happily if I know that you and Eleri will live.'

Rhianna stared at her for a moment, their eyes locked on each other. Behind them the Roman war-horns blared again, and there was the buzz of more arrows being fired.

'I will do my best to make sure of that,' said Rhianna, tears in her eyes.

'Farewell, Rhianna,' said Garwen. 'May the goddess always protect you.'

She pulled the reins and drove away without looking back. Rhianna watched her go, then she took Eleri's hand and ran up the slope with her. A few moments later they reached the first trees and went into the darkness beneath them. Garwen's words still rang in Rhianna's ears, and she knew they should keep running, as Garwen had said. But Rhianna couldn't leave yet – she had to see what was happening.

So she turned round, heading back in the direction they had come, pulling Eleri along behind her. But Eleri dragged her heels. 'Can't we just go?' she moaned.

'Soon, I promise,' said Rhianna. 'You don't have to watch anything...'

They reached the edge of the woods at last, Rhianna making sure they stayed in the shadows so they wouldn't be spotted. But she had a clear view into the valley, and saw that Garwen had reclaimed her place, her chariot once more out in front of the others, facing the Romans. Rhianna looked for the queen, and there she was, behind the war-host, still on the grassy mound with Tegan and Maeve. And beyond the mound were the wagons, all of them packed with excited women and children.

The Romans hadn't moved, but something else had changed. The Roman captives were no longer on their knees – they were lying in heaps, and even at such a distance Rhianna could see the dark bloodstains on their clothes. She felt the fiery bile in her stomach rising up her throat and thought she was going to be sick. But then the chariots suddenly leaped forward, Garwen leading the charge up the valley.

The chariots swept over the grass, a rolling wave of thunder, the pounding of hoofbeats and the rumbling of wheels echoing off the slopes.

Behind them came the war-host, thousands of warriors running and screaming war cries, the blades of their swords and spears gleaming like fallen stars. Yet the Romans stood motionless and silent, and Rhianna couldn't help feeling it made them even more terrifying.

Suddenly the war-horns blared again, and the Romans moved at last, a second line of soldiers stepping through the front rank. Each of these men threw a spear and a cloud of slim wood shafts and deadly metal rose over the chariots... then fell and caused chaos. Wounded horses went down, pulling their chariots over, and others crashed into them. Rhianna saw drivers sent flying, or dragged along tangled in their reins, and the charge soon floundered in a mass of smashed wood and dying flesh.

The war-host was thrown into confusion, most of the warriors bunching up behind the wrecked chariots, the rest running into them. Yet again the war-horns blew, and the Roman front line began to advance steadily, each soldier banging his sword on his shield. Rhianna heard more hoofbeats – but this time it was the Roman cavalry. They must have been hiding beyond the opposite slope, she thought, as she watched in horror as they came galloping over it and crashed into the flank of the war-host.

A third line of Romans emerged now, fanning out towards the other slope. They attacked the war-host on the flank facing the woods, below Rhianna and Eleri. Blades rose and fell as the fighting grew more intense, and Rhianna looked away at last.

Then she took Eleri's hand and they ran off between the trees.

* * *

They stayed in the woods that night and all the next day, hiding in a hole beneath the roots of an oak tree felled by a winter storm. Rhianna covered the hole with branches and leaves and they sat huddled together, staying quiet, listening to distant voices, running footsteps, pounding hoofbeats and the jingle of harness and weapons. On the second day they heard nothing and Rhianna decided they could risk leaving.

It was a mistake. They came to a clearing and walked straight into a Roman patrol, fifty soldiers sweeping the woods for anyone trying to escape from the battlefield. Rhianna yelled at Eleri to run, but rough Roman hands grabbed them and they soon found themselves in a group of prisoners being marched to the Roman camp. Now Rhianna told herself they were truly doomed – there was no way out this time.

Then something amazing happened, and the world changed once more.

When they reached the camp Rhianna saw that it was surrounded by a ditch and a mound topped with a palisade of sharpened wooden stakes. They were taken inside, along a track between lines of tents, and herded like animals into a corral. It was packed with prisoners and guarded by hard-eyed Roman soldiers. Beyond them two more Romans were passing, a woman with a young girl. The woman turned as if by chance and looked at Rhianna – and they recognised each other instantly.

Her name was Camilla, and as she kept saying, she could never thank Rhianna enough for saving her and her daughter. Camilla was married to a certain Titus Ligerius Macro, a 'tribune who served Paulinus himself'. Rhianna had no idea what all that meant, but it seemed Macro was important enough to have her and Eleri set free. By the end of that day they were in Camilla's tent, eating Roman bean stew and bread. Camilla's daughter Aemilia sat next to Eleri, and it was soon clear the two girls enjoyed each other's company.

Later, when Eleri and Aemilia were asleep, Camilla and Rhianna talked. It turned out that Camilla had lived in Britannia for many years. Her father was a soldier and had come with the invasion force, then married a girl from one of the tribes of the south coast, the Regni – which explained why Camilla spoke a tongue Rhianna could understand. Camilla had married Titus and they had settled in Camulodunum.

'Titus went with Paulinus to Mona,' said Camilla. 'We didn't expect the tribes to rebel – it was a complete surprise. The worst thing was knowing that I could do nothing to protect Aemilia. But you know all about that, don't you, Rhianna?'

'Yes, I suppose so,' said Rhianna. 'Tell me, what happened in the battle?'

Camilla looked at her, then shrugged. 'Titus says it was a great slaughter. Your warriors were trapped between our soldiers and the line of their own wagons blocking the way out of the valley. Some managed to escape, but like you, they didn't get far.'

'What will Paulinus do with them?' said Rhianna, thinking of the prisoners.

'They will be sold as slaves. And before you ask, I don't think even Titus could persuade Paulinus to free any more. They have rebelled against Rome, and the Emperor will want him to make an example of them. There will be more suffering to come as well, in the homelands of the tribes – Paulinus plans to lay them waste.'

Rhianna closed her eyes and pictured the Royal Place in her mind, the tracks busy with people, the Meeting Ground crowded for the Summer Gathering or the Winter Solstice. She thought of Magunna and Segovax, and Viducos and Cara and their sons, and Cumenal and Andorix and their families, of Garwen lying under her smashed chariot. All gone now, like the dawn mist burned off by the sun when it rises.

'What about the queen and her daughters?' she said, opening her eyes.

'They are dead,' Camilla said softly, holding Rhianna's hand. 'According to Titus they took poison rather than be captured. They were wise to do so, I feel.'

Rhianna remembered the jars and pots and dried herbs hanging in the rafters of the Queen's House, and Boudica's skill with healing potions and salves. Of course the queen could make poisons too, she realised. There was a dark side to many things.

'And what about Eleri and me?' said Rhianna. 'Where are we to find a home?'

'Why, you must come and live with us,' said Camilla with a warm smile. 'We are going to stay with my mother and father. They have a farm near Anderida, on the south coast. I owe you more than I can ever repay, so please say yes…'

Rhianna met her gaze and thought for a moment. Then she nodded.

This time it really was the right thing to do.

Historical Note

The people living in the islands of Britannia before the Romans came had a rich and complex way of life. They were farmers and warriors, worshipped their own gods and goddesses, and they must have had many myths and legends to explain the world and their past. But they left no written records, so all we know about them comes to us from the discoveries of archaeologists and from what the Romans said about them.

The Romans did write things down – and one Roman in particular wrote about Boudica and her rebellion. His name was Publius Cornelius Tacitus, he lived in the first century CE, and his wife's father – Gnaeus Julius Agricola – served with Suetonius Paulinus, the governor of Britannia during the revolt. So it's likely that Tacitus got most of his information from Agricola, who saw a lot of it first-hand.

Tacitus says that Boudica was tall, had tawny, waist-length hair and a loud voice. He also describes the horrific things that Boudica's war-host did to the Romans living in the three cities that she captured and burned. There is an old saying that only the winners write history, and many people have said we can't really know the truth of what happened in Boudica's revolt because we don't know her side of the story. Yet there's no doubt that three cities were burned to the ground – in each of them, archaeologists have found a layer of ash they can date to the revolt.

The Romans were brutal themselves – they invaded many other countries, crushed all opposition, and treated those who rebelled against them very harshly. The Roman Empire was rich and powerful, but it was based on slavery.

It took enormous courage to rise against them, and Boudica must have been a terrific leader. But it has always seemed to me that there was something dark about her rebellion. She released all the hatred of a conquered people for their oppressors, and that led to terrible things. In the end it destroyed her tribe, and the other tribes that rose with her. Paulinus laid waste their lands, and the Iceni, the Trinovantes and the Catuvellauni disappeared from history. Eventually Britannia settled down as a Roman province, and remained in the Roman Empire until it began to fall apart four hundred years later.

One thing we do know about the Iceni is that unlike other British tribes, they don't appear to have been dominated by the Druids. So it could be that they worshipped the 'triple goddess' I've written about in this story – there is certainly evidence some tribes did. The Romans, however, believed that only men should have any real power, so religion might well have played a part in Boudica's revolt – on both sides.

Perhaps Rhianna continued to find comfort in a kind and loving goddess, and she and Eleri lived on and prospered. That's what I like to think, anyway...